DO I have to tell you we are still part of the Second Infantry Regiment? I represent *that*, don't I? And these men represent me? Survival is morale—and morale is pride! If I can't give them pride in anything else, I'll give them the pride to stand up and hate me in the open, and maybe it'll save their lives."

Also by Brian Garfield:

THE LAST HARD MEN   X2877 $1.75

SWEENY'S HONOR

Brian Garfield

FAWCETT CREST • NEW YORK

SWEENY'S HONOR

Published by Fawcett Crest Books, a unit of CBS Publications, the Consumer Publishing Division of CBS Inc.

Copyright © 1971 by Brian Garfield

ISBN: 0-449-24330-3

Printed in the United States of America

First Fawcett Crest printing: September 1980

10   9   8   7   6   5   4   3   2   1

INTRODUCTION

SWEENY'S HONOR

The ferryboat at Yuma Crossing on the Colorado River was operated peacefully for centuries by the Yuma Indians, from the days of the earliest Spanish explorations up to the time of the great California Gold Rush.

Then, in 1850, a gang of gringo outlaws took it away from them by force of arms.

The outlaws immediately raised toll charges to astronomical levels: they had a monopoly on the only practical river crossing in 500 miles. And since it was the peak of the Gold Rush, traffic was heavy and profits were enormous.

The Yuma tribe was not quick to anger; indeed, they displayed remarkable tolerance. But finally they rose in reprisal—killed fourteen outlaws and sent the other three packing. The three survivors escaped across the desert to San Diego, where they raised a hue and cry that was speedily picked up by newspapers and word-of-mouth. The "massacre" became a public issue, and the state of California soon sent out a ragtag company of militia to "avenge the murders" and "subdue the hostile savages." The militia destroyed the tribe's pumpkin crop, wounded a few Indians, and at the first sign of Indian outrage they retreated quickly to friendlier climes.

Nobody ever suggested the profitable ferry be given back to its original owners, the Yumas. Instead, a group of white businessmen organized a private company to reopen the ferry. Their demands for Army protection soon brought the U. S. 2nd Infantry Regiment out to the Yuma Crossing. An Army garrison was built on the site of the ruins of a Spanish mission, which the Indians had wiped out in 1781.

One of the regiment's officers was Lieutenant Thomas William Sweeny, born in Ireland on Christmas Day, 1820. . . .

ONE

In a poor mood I went down the slope, looking for Sweeny, loathing the heat and the Dutchman. Along the wide river a layer of sunset heat stirred close to the banks; it clouded the dust around my boots and swirled a mist on the brown surface of the Colorado. In the bottoms the brush slowed my pace, where the spring overflow had dried and left behind a treacherous footing of clay mud, cracked into cakes by the sun.

I followed the bend around toward the west, tipping the shako visor far down over my eyes against the red glare, and came to a tiny field that sprouted sickly tufts of new young corn, beans, pumpkins. I would have trampled across if I hadn't been under surveillance: Pascual's Yuma warriors kept sharp eyes on the vital seedlings. One of them, tall and naked, stood by the bank to my left with a *toketa* club balanced across his shoulder; and, accordingly, I made a point of walking carefully around the random-shaped edge of the field. The Indian returned his simmering attention to the ferryboat, creaking its way across the quarter-mile width of the Colorado on its guy ropes, poled by four of Lou Yaeger's hairy boatmen.

I pushed through the scrub willows and felt the heat: it pasted the shirt to my back, ran sweat into my eyes. It was worse down here; the bottoms stored it up like a furnace.

A woman came by with a bucket of woven grass, barefoot, moving with high-hipped grace. According to prevailing fashion she wore a rabbit-skin breechclout and a string of trader's beads, nothing more. She presented a proud brace of jutting brown breasts tipped with dark rosettes, drew my hungry attention, gave me a shy flirting laugh, and went by toward the village.

Close by the edge of the village I found Sweeny in the flood-bottom rushes, down on one knee, talking earnestly with old Pascual, discoursing in bad Spanish with wide sweeps of his arm. Pascual was intent, suspicious. I caught Sweeny's eye but he frowned a warning at me without interrupting his talk.

Antoine Leroux squatted in the background like a slumbering gray wolf. I joined him and watched Sweeny teach the old chief to make water look as if it was boiling by dropping seltzer salts in it. Antoine Leroux said to me, "A frinly gesture, dimonstratin' white man's medicine. H'are yew, Lieutenant?"

"Hot and rancid," I replied. "He just about done?"

"Jest about." Antoine's hair was pewter-gray, a wild, thick crop that stood out as if struck by lightning. He was fifty years old, half-French and half Mexican-Indian, and he looked all of it. His habitual expression was that of a man who had just smelled something distasteful; the long face was weathered, dour and wry, expressive of indescribable anguish. He said, "Ever little thang heps if it keeps 'em frinly."

"The Dutchman wants us," I said. "Let's bust this up."

"Gentle down, Lieutenant. Been mah sperience

8

when you fand a frinly Innun you smart to keep him that way. Maybe Tom's medicine will hep old Pascual stay chief. Otherwise some of them hotbloods bump the old gent aside, we get trouble up to the asshole."

I scowled at him and turned to look at the others. Pascual was a crickety old man with a coppery parchment face that looked as if it belonged on an old Roman coin. His abrupt outbursts of idiot giggling were part of a calculated pose—somebody must have told him the white men liked it best if he acted like fragile antique made childish by senility. I suppose it might have fooled the Dutchman. But I did not trust Pascual.

Sweeny sprinkled powder into the pot. The water sizzled and the old man cackled with delight. Sweeny, not fooled, stroked his beard and watched. He had a pipe clenched in his teeth and a merry glint in his dark eyes. Thin, tiny, black-bearded, he was my age, but his laugh made him younger. Four years ago at Cerro Gordo I had thought they'd knocked all the laughter out of him, but I was wrong; nothing could repress him. I had been scalded by that first meeting with him, the memory of it burned in as if by hot steel, and it still came back often: Sweeny on a pallet in a big tent full of carnage, his face bloodless white, his eyes hardly tracking, his right arm truncated below the shoulder by the surgeon's bloody saw. I had come to him bearing a macabre gift: Kearny had lost his left arm, had heard about Sweeny, and had sent me to that dismal field hospital in Mexico with all his left-hand dress gloves and a note full of gallows humor. Sweeny hadn't laughed then. But later he had.

That had been a thousand miles ago. Now Sweeny wore the empty right sleeve pinned up at his shoulder like a flag of defiance. He was laughing with Pascual as if he had never known pain.

9

The old Indian got up from his haunches, talking toothlessly. Sweeny pressed the bag of seltzer powders into his hand and Pascual came away clutching it, grinning. He favored Leroux and me with the grin and hurried into the village.

Before he spoke to me, Sweeny bit off a piece of plug tobacco and thumbed it down into his pipe, put a match to it and chugged out a disgusting cloud of smoke. "Well? Cat got your tongue? What disaster have we got this time?"

"Did I say a word?"

"The minute I saw your face," he said, "I knew the world had fallen down around your ankles."

Antoine Leroux was easy prey to Sweeny's erratic wit; he nearly collapsed. All I said was, "The Dutchman's holding court. You and I have been summoned."

"To come before the august presence," Sweeny said. "Has he found us out?"

"God knows. Hardcastle thinks he's decided to pull out."

"Out?"

Antoine exploded in a few choice phrases. Sweeny rubbed the back of his neck and squinted. "Balls. Pull out of here now?"

Antoine said, "What about the fuckin' ferryboat?"

"Come on," I said, and stepped off.

Sweeny batted through the brush beside me, sucking his pipe, his eyes agleam with suspicion. "What kind of shape is the darlin' Major in? Treating his wounds with alcohol again?"

"I don't know. I didn't see him. Hardcastle said he was puffed up full of resolve."

Sweeny said, "I will bet he looks like a seasick passenger who can't get the porthole open. Wouldn't it be a parfit time to paint the wagon mules pink and char-

10

treuse, and herd them through his tent?" His leer was obscene.

Leroux began to shake with silent laughter that developed into an agony of mirth: he hopped around in a circle behind us with his long homely face twisted by the pain of a thousand tortures. His big feet flapped like paddles. Finally he caught up with us, short of breath. "Where the hell you fixin' to fand pink paint out cheer?"

"Pascual ought to know how to make it." Sweeny made an impudent gesture toward the top of the bluff with a distended finger. He began to turn back toward the village but I grabbed his arm. He glared at me. "What's the matter with you?"

"You heard what I said. He's holding an audience—he wants us there."

"Balls. By now he doesn't even remember why he wanted us."

Antoine said, "Naw. Heintzelman gives awders, drunk or otherwise, you soldier boys bound to obey them."

Sweeny came along reluctantly. We started up the slope of the bluff and Antoine said, "Sweet Christ, he pulls out rat nah, you gonna have yoseff one bitch of a little old uprising."

"Never let it be said," Sweeny remarked loftily, "that the mind of Major Samuel P. Heintzelman could be swayed by such a minuscule item as an Indian uprising."

"Shee-yit," said Antoine.

We climbed toward the stockade, up the backside of the bluff, which was the only practical approach. Up in the corner blockhouse two sleepy soldiers stood guard over our single artillery piece, the diminutive brass twelve-pounder. We had floated the logs downriver all the way from the Black Canyon, and on this brushy, arid hill the pole stockade made an incongruous shape against the sky. The Indians had got used to it faster than I had; it still looked out of place to me, so that I had no trouble visualizing it crumbling into powder dust like everything else on this desert: it was like an unnatural growth, risking Nature's wrath by displeasing her.

I felt uneasy. I said to Sweeny, "Suppose the Dutchman's found out about the charges we filed?"

Sweeny said, "Careful you don't worry yourself into an untimely grave, Edward."

"Take it seriously, for once," I insisted. "Or didn't you read what you were signing when we drew them up?"

Sweeny was astonished. "*Read* them?"

"Then you'd withdraw them if he put pressure on?"

It brought him around; his face changed and he said in a different voice, "No—no."

"That's what I thought."

He didn't say anything more before we reached the post. The bored sentry at the gate was matching knife-throws with a Yuma warrior who whooped every time he scored a point. We took the sentry's salute and went inside, in twilight, and Antoine said immediately, "Sweet Christ."

The garrison, bedouin-style tents covered by thatched sun-sheds, was full of busy, active motion—troopers scurrying back and forth with burdens, stripped down to their gray flannel pullovers and galluses, sleeves rolled up, streaming sweat, converging in confused knots around the wagon corrals. Loud oaths carried across the flat of the parade ground, sergeants bellowing orders. I had never seen anything like it. "What the hell?"

12

Antoine said, "Begins to look lak Hardcastle was rat."

Sweeny said, "Bite your tongue, Antoine."

That was when Magruder and Bean erupted from a tent in our path, locked together in combat. Grunting, cursing, wrestling, they rolled across the hardpan. It brought me up short. Antoine said, "Jesus Christ." I took a step forward to put a stop to it—but Sweeny put out a detaining hand:

"Let them be having their fun."

They were Sweeny's men, not mine. I scowled at him. The privates pummeled each other, oblivious, and I said to Sweeny, "Why don't you discipline them once in a while? They could use a few inhibitions."

"Fuck discipline. You silly West Pointer. They came out here for a fight, didn't they?"

Magruder and Bean heaved to their feet and went at each other with fists. Antoine, yawning, picked a wide path around them and strolled toward the Major's tent at the end of the compound. Sweeny said, "Get your left up, Magruder. No, Jesus, your *other* left!"

I said, "You ridiculous mick," and went after Antoine, refusing to look back. I heard someone strike a loud blow, like the smack of the flat of a cleaver against beefsteak. Sweeny's loud laugh rang across the post; I heard a howl and Bean's hoarse voice: "Lord Christ, all right. *All right*—enough!"

Sweeny came along and remarked to me, "If you don't let them blow off steam now and then they tend to boil over."

Hardcastle was lying in wait near the Dutchman's tent, worry on his big red face. Sweeny greeted him with good cheer: "My good Captain."

Hardcastle cleared his throat and said, in a voice

meant to carry no farther than our ears, "You're late, I'm nervous, and he's fit to be tied."

Foolishly I said, "What's all the activity?"

"Can't you see for yourself?"

"I was hoping it was a mirage."

Sweeny said, "And so we're packing it up, are we?"

Hardcastle's whisper was conspiratorial. "He's about to run out of whisky and he wants to get back to the fleshpots of San Diego."

"Shee-yit," said Antoine.

Hardcastle said, "Pulling out at first light. You'd better get in there—he wants all three of you in the very worst way."

I said, "What's his condition?"

"Dangerously sober."

I exchanged glances with Sweeny and Antoine. Hardcastle rolled his eyes and walked away, with Sweeny hissing at him, "Craven coward!" He made a face and walked to the tent, stamped his feet and said in a loud voice, "Sir, Lieutenants Sweeny and Murray. And Scout Leroux."

"Get your asses in here," the Dutchman roared from within. His voice was alarmingly clear and firm.

I followed Sweeny inside under the flap. Antoine trailed in after us and ranged himself by the entrance as if ready to bolt.

The Dutchman was at his camp table with his large purple face propped up in his palm. His eyes were not bloodshot, they appeared to be in focus, and he was clearly in one of his sarcastic moods. "About goddamn time," he snapped. "Mister Sweeny, considering the Mexican War was of relatively brief duration, how is it you managed to get there promptly enough to get your arm blown off?"

14

"One would suppose the Mexicans thought I was worth waiting for, sir."

Antoine snickered. The Dutchman silenced it with a savage look. The lamp on the camp table threw his face into harsh relief when he sat back. He was half-bald, hair making a bushy line across the top of his head from ear to ear—he always looked more like a bartender than an officer. He said to Sweeny, "I wish it had been your head."

Antoine said, "You making a fucking big mistake. You can't pull out rat nah—you do, and you get ever last one of them ferryboat men killed, just as sure and certain as they's a hole in your ass."

The Major gave him a pained look. Finally he emitted a large sigh, swung his feet to the floor, sat up, scratched his chest, and said, "Horse shit."

"Naw," Antoine said.

The Major's unhappy glance roved from face to face. "For no good reason that I can think of," he said, "I'll tell you what I have already told those officers who were kind enough to report here an hour ago when summoned. The facts are perhaps so simple that even your uncluttered brains can absorb them. One: Our last supply train had to be abandoned in the dunes forty miles west of here because the wagons sank up to their bottoms in sand."

Sweeny said, sotto voce, "How much whisky was aboard?"

If the Major heard it he ignored it. He went on: "Two: The troops are on half-rations and I see no prospect for relief. Three: One reason we were sent here was to place the regiment as far as possible from the gold-fields, so we could minimize desertions from the ranks. As of this morning's roll call, fifty-eight men have disappeared from this post in the past five months. Obviously that example of War Department genius was faulty somewhere. Four: The primary reason we were sent here was to protect the ferryboat. After the past five months' experience with that old fool Pascual it seems clear to me a squad of armed men, let alone an entire regiment, could protect the ferry damn well."

Antoine gave a derisive snort. "I always knowed you had your brains up your ass."

The Major reared back on his dignity. "I don't like your tone, Antoine. You keep a civil tongue in your head."

"I'm a civilian."

"Thank God."

"I got a right to speak my piece."

"Fine. Speak it somewhere else."

"I got a right here."

"Hah! I can have you put off Army property any time."

"I expeck you could. Only then you got to fand yoseff somebody else to guide you acrosst the dunes." Antoine's face settled into a benign agony which passed for smugness. I saw Sweeny grin behind his hand before he put the pipe back in his mouth.

The Major said, "I don't intend to leave the boat crews unprotected. But I can't keep the regiment supplied here. There's only one thing to do—and we're doing it. I'm leaving a detachment here to defend the crossing, and I'll leave all the supplies I can spare. When we reach San Diego I'll send a supply column back, with Antoine to guide the wagons."

Antoine said, "How big a detaichment you gonna leave?"

"Big enough."

"Company size, my judgment. Otherwise they git attackted just once by them Innuns and they git dead."

"Horse shit. These savages haven't got guns. A dozen well-armed men will do—I can't provide supplies for more."

"Shee-yit, you cain't——"

"I can. By God I can. Shut up, Antoine. You're dismissed. Get out of here."

When Antoine glanced at Sweeny I saw Sweeny shake his head slightly. Antoine wheeled with a curse and tramped out.

The Dutchman cocked his head, reassuring himself Antoine had gone beyond earshot. Then he sat back at the camp table and steepled his fingers. "What, no explosion of remarks from you two? You've never approved of a single decision of mine in the past and I'm sure this is no exception. Well?"

Sweeny said, "You're in command here."

"How kind of you to recall. You, Murray?"

"Would anything I say change your mind?"

"Not goddamn likely."

"Well, then."

He blinked and put his palms down on the table. "Indeed. Think of that." He screwed his face up in a squint, which he directed at Sweeny. "Peculiar, to say the least, when suddenly you two loudmouthed crows have nothing at all to say."

I said, stiff and arch, "Is that all, sir?"

He began to smile, which was when the small hairs on the back of my neck began to crawl. He said, "Not quite." His smile grew, became a smirk, and settled on his face as if engraved. "Your orders, gentlemen," he breathed.

Sweeny looked at me. I couldn't fathom his expression.

The Major said, "Murray, you'll march with the regiment as far as Vallecito Station on the far side of the

17

dunes. I'm leaving you there with a detachment of four privates to render protection and assistance to travelers. Under no circumstances will you venture farther than ten miles west of your duty post. Is that understood?"

I only glared at him. He kept smiling sweetly; he said, "You, Sweeny. You will remain here at Yuma Crossing with a noncommissioned officer and nine enlisted men until further notice. Under no circumstances will you venture west of the dunes. Your orders are to prevent hostiles from harassing the ferry company."

Sweeny made no reply. I exploded. "You're an honest-to-God bastard."

"Sir," the Dutchman prompted quietly.

"Sir."

I said, "It's a cheap trick and you won't get away with it. Sir."

"On the contrary. It's an honor any young officer would jump at. Think of the opportunities for glory, gentlemen. The chance to go down in history, valiantly defending your posts against hordes of whooping savages. Why, I almost wish I was young enough to do it myself."

"Of course you do," I said. "Sir."

He smirked. "I didn't think you'd like it much. But one good turn does deserve another in kind, don't you think?"

I looked at Sweeny.

The Major snorted. "Did you think you could keep it from me forever? What you must think of me!"

Sweeny said, "We do our best not to."

"Not to what?"

"Think of you. Sir."

Heintzelman went back to his cot, eased himself

18

down onto it and spoke in the direction of the low tent ceiling. "I'm sure I could arrange your transfers to a desirable garrison back East. But one favor deserves another in kind, as I said." He rolled his head toward his shoulder until he could look at both of us. "Naturally I've delayed the charges in channels by using what small influence I possess with General Smith's staff. Maybe I've got enough influence up there to get them quashed altogether, but I'd have to scuttle around a lot and I'd rather not bother. You understand? I'm holding out an olive branch. I'm willing to let bygones be bygones if you two will drop the charges."

"Are you now," Sweeny said.

"Everyone this side of Jefferson Barracks knows the reputation you two have for exuberance and fun-loving zeal. I'm sure all you need to do is admit you were both, ah, under the influence of Demon Rum at the time you drew up the charges against me. You'll suffer no loss of face."

A cloud of smoke floated free from Sweeny's pipe. "No," he said.

"No, what?"

"No, sir. The charges stand."

The Major's inquiring glance shifted to me. I said, "I'm the one who drew them up. Nothing's changed my mind. Sir."

The Major shrugged and his glance wandered away. His chin came to rest on his chest. He had a habit of looking down at himself, perhaps out of uncertainty as to whether his fly was buttoned, or perhaps just making sure his body was still there. He sighed. "You two have got real balls, I'll say that. You realize this is your last chance to back out of this stupidity? A lark's a lark, and I hold no hard feelings when there's a good joke at my expense. But carry it beyond here and I'll use every power I have to crush both of you into powder."

I said, "Let's get one thing straight, sir. The charges are true."

"I admit nothing. And you know damn well the risk a junior runs when he makes a charge against a superior. Two shavetail lieutenants against a respected Army major—think about it."

"Two seasoned, veteran regular army officers," I said through my teeth, "against a political hack who got his oak leaves from friends in high places. You don't expect we'll fail to point that out in court, do you, sir?"

Momentarily his head lifted off the cushion and he glowered at me. But after a moment he thought better of it and lay back; he only said mildly, "Do let me know if you change your minds about it."

Sweeny sucked his pipe, imbecilely calm. Full of hot rage, I couldn't control my trembling muscles. The Dutchman said in a pleasant way, "Just one other thing, Sweeny. I want you to keep tabs on the number of fare-paying passengers the ferry carries across the river. Every day until further notice."

I said, "To make sure your cutthroat partners don't cheat you of your share?"

"Nonsense," he purred. "I've got to have facts and figures for my reports to higher command, that's all. Sweeny?"

"What?"

"You haven't said a word. Are you listening?"

"Avidly."

"Haven't you any comment? It's the first time I've seen you speechless."

"Why, I'd just as soon be saving all that for your trial," Sweeny said. His dark eyes, reflecting lamplight, glittered frostily through the rancid cloud of pipe smoke.

The Major smiled lazily at the ceiling. "I am confident," he murmured, "that you won't live long enough to see me come to trial. You may go now, both of you— you're dismissed."

Outside the tent, in closing-down dusk, a hot breeze raked my cheeks. There was a lot of bawling and swearing, men packing up, rushing by as we walked away from the Dutchman's tent. I wheeled to confront Sweeny and barked at him in pique: "He'll murder both of us. He'll get you killed and then he'll order me back here to take your place."

"Sure and indubitably," Sweeny said in his brogue. His pipe had gone out; he knocked it against the heel of his boot.

I said, "I am seriously thinking about strangling him."

"And hang for it? Or perhaps you'd rather disobey the orders and hang for mutiny."

I said, "Don't you ever take anything seriously?"

"Now and again. Don't sweat so much, Edward. Hardcastle will make sure the charges don't get lost in the dust behind some lard-ass subaltern's desk. You and I only have to wait—it'll be a while, there's always channels to go through, but we'll spike him. Stick it out, Ed, me friend, and we'll prove which of us are the better men. Just stay alive and enjoy as much of it as you can."

"And how much d'you think that'll be—and for how long, Tom? You with ten men and the Yumas with four hundred, not to mention God knows how many unfriendly Yavapais upriver."

"I'll just have to be keeping Pascual happy, won't I?"

21

Sweeny rammed the pipe through his belt like a pistol and clapped me on the arm. "All in due time. Damn it, Ed, what have *you* to complain about? They've got trees at Vallecito Station. Faith and begorra—trees and good food and fat, healthy women. Take your pleasures where you can; don't be clouding the day with gloom. Methinks you scowl too much."

"I'll smile when I see that besotted bastard's head on a platter."

Sweeny laughed.

TWO

Vallecito Station was a place to be seen in moonlight. By day it left much to be desired. I stood just outside the ramshackle wagon shed where my four soldiers were billeted, angling my face into the faint miasmic breeze and squinting against the unfriendly sun. Trooper Betts said, "Orders for the day, Lieutenant?"

The four of them slouched hipshot in the shade. Betts was hard-bitten, brown-bearded, a man who kept his own counsel and gave away nothing of his personality; it was possible he had joined the Army to escape the law somewhere—I might have been wrong but he left that impression. He was closemouthed but not at all surly like the other three, who favored me with crabby glances and made it clear they hated the heat, the place, the Army, and me.

In the past week I had settled them in and shaken them down. Now I had to think of something to keep them busy.

I said to Betts, "There's loose lumber lying around behind the buildings. See if you can gather up enough to build a shower bath in back of the wagon shed."

One of the men turned his head and spat. Nobody had any other comment, but I tried to gentle them down: "I don't care if you're clean or dirty. But a shower now and then can cool a man down and make this place easier to live in. We're standing on top of a sulphur mineral spring and we may as well make use of it."

They shuffled off to work and I went up to the porch of the store, dipped a drink out of the clay water *olla* that hung in a rope net under the rafters, and sat down on the step, feeling dismal. Posted out to nowhere by the Dutchman's vindictive spite. I had tried to make the best of it, but I was just as bored and resentful as the four troopers and there wasn't much to be done about it. Every morning I was surprised to find they hadn't slipped away during the night: perhaps the heat filled them with too much dispirited listlessness to leave room for thoughts of flight.

The trees here were sparse and stunted, the company dull, the grass full of chiggers, ants, scorpions, and manure. The only excuse for the station's existence was its mineral spring. A parboiled paradise at best. There was a litter of salt-grass sod buildings constructed across the trail and we had travelers coming through at a steady rate, westbound toward the coastal trails that would take them north to the gold country. None of them reported any contact with Indians, which was not surprising in view of the fact that the only Indians in the region lived in a small missionized community a quarter mile up the road; they supported themselves mainly by a lackadaisical industry in roadside prostitution—Sweeny's "fat, healthy women." Their health in fact was open to question—one of the station hostlers complained of the crabs—and hence I personally was discouraged from sampling their wares, although Betts and the men made frequent hikes to the village.

The station's proprietor came out onto the store porch and muttered, "Good morning," and I grunted in response. He was a tall man of piratical mien and uncertain antecedents who went by the name of Juan

24

Largo, which translated into Long John. His family name had been left behind, together with his history, on an obscure backtrail. Perhaps he enjoyed playing the role of Man of Mystery, but he wasn't of much interest to me, since the one dominant interest in his life was one I did not share: gambling.

He went down the steps past me and strode toward the corrals, tramping his shadow into the ground. I watched him, because there was nothing else to look at. Juan Largo operated the trading post, ran small flocks of sheep and goats, and was disliked. I hadn't exchanged a hundred words with him in the week; he had lost all interest in me as soon as he had discovered I wasn't a card player. He devoted most of his time to solitaire, the rest of it to criticizing his employees and persuading travelers to gamble with him. He drank a good deal, and he left the running of the store to a red-haired woman named Abigail Marshall, a formidable young creature who carried a seven-shot pepperbox pistol in her sash and discouraged all male approaches with fierce looks and no-nonsense defiance. She called herself Mrs. Marshall and lived alone in a sod cabin behind the store. She kept house for Juan Largo but whether the relationship went beyond that I could not tell.

Betts reported the shower bath built at noon, and in the afternoon I borrowed five saddle-mules to take the men out on a reconnaissance patrol. We crossed paths with a party of five Mexicans driving a large flock of sheep; they had seen no Indians and declined my halfhearted offer of an escort to Calexico. We returned to the station at six with sweat streaming down our faces.

The streaky lemon sunlight pearled the dust hanging in the air. With nothing better to do, I stripped and stepped into the shower enclosure, inspected the workmanship, and worked the pump handle. Water sprayed out of the sieved bucket above my head. I scrubbed away the caked dust, stepped outside and reached up for the towel, and froze.

Abigail Marshall had come in sight carrying a bucket of cooking fats and wood ashes for making soap. We stared at each other until I felt myself blush. She put the bucket down without hurry, straightened, palmed the long red hair back from her face, looked me up and down, and burst into lusty laughter.

I snatched the towel down and wrapped it around my middle. The neat laughing teeth were gritted white against her tan face; her big bawdy guffawing rang through the air and made me cringe. I put my hat on and threw my uniform across my arm, picked up my boots and walked toward my quarters.

I had to go past her into the alley between the wagon shed and the store. She didn't step aside. I stopped. She was grinning openly when she said, "That's a mean scar across your hip, Lieutenant."

"Aeah," I said through my teeth, and began to edge past her. I could see one bright laughing eye through the wild tumble of her hair. The handle of the pepperbox pistol stuck out of her sash. Arch and stiff, I circled past and went on to my quarters. When I went inside my cheeks were stinging as if with heat rash.

Every time we crossed paths in the next two days I turned crimson and she laughed. I began to go to extraordinary lengths to avoid her; her ridicule was merciless and I had no defense against it. I began to dislike her passionately.

Two Texans named Morgan and Hines came plodding in from the west with four herders and fifteen hundred sheep bound for the gold camps. They told me they had had trouble at Yuma Crossing.

"Yaeger brung the sheep acrosst the river 'thout no trouble," Hines said, "but that one-armed Lieutenant had to hold a hunnerd goddamn Innuns at bay with that little brass cannon of his'n, otherwise we'd never of got thew."

"Seems they had a little off-season flood," Morgan explained, ripping off a mouthful from a mutton joint with his teeth. "Wiped out the Innuns' seedling crops. Hard to tell which was hungrier—the Innuns or the soldier boys. We give six head of sheep to the Lieutenant there, but that won't last 'em long."

"Specially considering the Lieutenant turned rat around and give three of the sheep to the Innun chief," Hines said dryly. "What for did he have to go and do that?"

After supper they went off to their overnight camp and I went out and stood in the station street, looking east at the hills as if my burning gaze could penetrate the night across the sixty sandy miles to the Yuma Crossing. I had thought about Sweeny frequently in the past three weeks, wondered and hoped; now I could see the bleak truth. The Dutchman's scheme was working. Sweeny was in bad trouble.

Abigail Marshall was on the store porch, heating wax to seal preserves in glass jars. She called my name and I could not pretend I hadn't heard. Feeling the flush crawl up my neck I turned toward her and approached suspiciously, staying clear of the fan of lamplight that splashed out through the open door.

"Come up and sit down, Lieutenant. I won't jump you."

"May I have that in writing?"

27

"Come on, then. I promise I won't laugh." But her face was full of mischief.

"I suppose I've acted like a fool," I said awkwardly. I climbed the steps and sat down in the rough-hewn rocker.

"Would you like a drink?"

I glanced up at the water *olla,* suspended in its rope net. She said, "Not that. I've got some fair drinking whisky inside."

She pushed her lower lip forward to blow hair off her forehead; she had a smoky voice and pale, dramatic eyes that watched me with elusive mockery. The dust was in my teeth; I said, "I could use it."

She put down her work and stood up to go inside. I watched her overtly. She was long-boned tall but she had good quivery breasts and a provocatively outflaring rump. Her face was curiously delicate without being at all fragile; it was in the exquisite placement of fine bones, the clean lines of jaw and cheeks, the triangular shape of her eyes—eyes which, in the lamplight, had the startling brilliance of gemstones, blue-flecked gray against the heavy, rich warmth of color in her hair and in her skin, which held a peppering of freckles under the weather-tan. She was vibrant, animated, vital, hearty, and no young child of the woods.

She disappeared inside, leaving me with humid interest, and shortly returned with an amber bottle and two coffee mugs. "Been a long time since I've seen a drinking glass," she said, pulling the cork with her teeth and splashing whisky into the mugs. She handed me mine, settled in her seat and lifted the mug in toast. *"Salud, pesos y amor, y tiempo para gustarlos."* Health, money and love, and time to enjoy them.

"Fine sentiments," I said. The bouquet was surprising; the whisky was excellent. "Smooth drink, a quiet evening, a beautiful woman's company. What more can a man ask?"

"Why don't you tell me, Lieutenant?"

"Meaning no insult, I'd just as soon be in cooler country. Where'd this whisky come from?"

"It was my husband's."

I stiffened.

She said distinctly, "My husband died a year ago next month. Of smallpox."

"I'm sorry."

"Why? You never even met him."

"For you, not for him. The dead don't need sympathy."

"Neither do I," she said. "George was a good man, about your size, but he had a weakness for gambling. Juan Largo showed up one day and that was that. My husband and I used to run this place together, but Juan Largo won this place from George and George went off to San Diego to see about raising money to start again. He stopped over at Warner's Ranch and the smallpox took him there."

She astonished me by her forthrightness—she had not spoken to me before, except of inconsequential things.

The whisky moved like a soft warm hand over the fibers of my body. I said, "Why did you stay here afterward?"

She seemed to hesitate; finally she said, "No money to go anywhere, and nowhere to go."

"Back home?"

"I have no home to go back to. It's just as well, there's no advantage in going back to things."

"This isn't an easy country for women."

"None of them are easy," she said, and the voice she used made me certain there were things in her past

29

she wanted forgotten. It occurred to me her answers had been vague; it was possible she remained here because she needed a refuge, a hiding place.

Tiny drops of sweat beaded her hairline; it might have been the heat, but then again it might have been nerves, and I still resented her earlier mockeries enough to seek revenge. I said, "Maybe there's something you're afraid to go back and face."

"You're impertinent," she riposted, "and presumptuous. But I suppose I deserve it. I've behaved badly toward you and·I apologize. Will you accept it?"

"All right."

"Thank you. You know, you've got a curious accent. You're from the South—what part of it?"

"Maryland. One of those little towns whose existence you define by saying it's eighteen miles from Baltimore."

"I picture a horsey plantation, Roman columns on the porch and a lot of black slaves."

I laughed. "Nothing like that. My father was a tailor."

"And so you joined the Army," she said. "Tell me about yourself, why don't you?"

"Why? Just for conversation? It's not very exciting."

"But I want to know all about you before I can decide."

"Decide what?" I asked, feeling uneasy.

She lifted one shoulder an inch. "Whether or not to put you on my list of people I'm talking to," she replied, and laughed to make sure I would see it was a joke. "Lieutenant Edward Murray, the son of a tailor in Maryland. Go on—tell me the rest." She gave me an intimate smile, but the mockery was still in the background.

"For three weeks," I said, "you've paid no more mind

30

to me than to one of those mules out there. What's changed that?"

"Perhaps I wanted to take the time to see how you sized up. You have to be careful about people out here, you know."

"What do you want of me?"

"You might start by telling me why you're in that uniform. Is it that you want to become a general?"

Oh, to hell with it, I thought. I settled back and drank some whisky and let my eyes rest against her. Her thick hair gathered light from the doorway. She accepted my appraisal, casual and unselfconscious. I said, "I suppose all of us want to become generals. That's what the game's all about. But it doesn't look as if I'll make it."

"Because you're stuck out here in this place?"

"Partly. Mostly because my friend and I filed charges against our commanding officer, and that's not always the best way to make friends in high places."

"I see. What sort of charges did you make?"

"It's a long story."

"I've got time," she said.

And so I told her about Sweeny and me and the Dutchman—how the Oatman party had been massacred on the Gila because Heintzelman wouldn't let Sweeny and me take a company upriver to escort them. He had been drunk; he had said to me, "Why bother?" He had only given protection to parties wealthy enough to pay him for it.

I said, "There are four or five specifications. Negligence, dereliction of duty, drunk on duty, and conflict-of-interests, because he takes pay for what he's supposed to do anyway from the people who own the ferry and from the travelers he's supposed to protect."

"And that's why he left you and your friend out here?"

"If he let us go back to San Diego, he knows we'd push the thing through and bring him into court. He's got to keep us out of the way long enough for him to bury the charges. And I guess he hopes we'll both get killed out here—he said as much."

"How could you be killed here? There's never been a hostile Indian in this part of California."

"Plenty of them at Yuma Crossing. If they kill Tom Sweeny the Major will order me back there to take his place."

I thought of Sweeny, always ready with a humorous remark and a bawdy laugh and, feeling miserable, I reached for the whisky bottle.

I was losing track of dates of the calendar but it was somewhere toward the middle of July when I took my four troopers out on a mounted patrol and, returning to the station, met a party of pilgrims making night camp outside the compound. They were bound for the diggings, armed with yellowing clippings from San Francisco papers heralding new discoveries in the Sacramento hills.

I kept close watch on my troopers that night. If they had been regulars I wouldn't have worried, but the Dutchman had assigned the worst of the regiment to Sweeny and me, and these four were irregulars who'd been conscripted by shanghai press-gangs in San Diego—not a bad lot but their discipline wasn't to be depended on.

The pilgrims hurried on in the morning, propelled by gold-fever, and my men watched them go with thoughtful interest. I kept them busy the rest of the day, kept them close at hand, and hoped to exhaust them beyond temptation. In the evening I saw them bedded down, and headed myself to the trading-post porch where by now an evening cup of whisky with the Widow Marshall was daily ritual.

"Goddamn it," she greeted me, "I want to make the world rattle a little before I die, Edward."

"I'm sure you do," I said, sitting down and reaching for the waiting mug.

She brooded at me. Her lips were parted, moist and heavy in repose, warm and generous when she forgot to be strict. I had come to know the shifting expressions of her fine-boned face, the different angles and shadows. There was strength and beauty in them. She had changed my concept of beauty; I no longer thought of her as frightening and formidable. Her forthright vulgarity had its own charm.

She said, "Tell me the happiest time you've ever had."

"I don't know," I replied. "I hope I haven't had it yet."

"Good for you," she applauded. "Tell me something else, then. Why aren't you married?"

"You're a blunt inquisitor sometimes, Abby."

"I haven't got time or patience to waste on roundabout rigamarole. Why aren't you married?"

"Oh, for God's sake!"

She grinned unabashedly.

I said, "If you've got to know, I'm unmarried because I'm ugly, undependable, and never found a girl who thought my face would be worth looking at across a breakfast table for forty years."

"You're not ugly," she retorted. "You've got a strong face—you look like a young Andrew Jackson."

"That's just the trouble."

"It didn't keep *him* from getting married."

33

"Look, why don't we just forget the subject?"

"All right," she said, teasing me with her grin. "I'll ask you something else, then. Where'd you get that scar on your hip?"

I felt my cheeks sting with color. I said, "In the Mexican War. Where'd you get yours?"

"Mine? My what?"

"Scars."

She paused contemplatively. A wind came up and her long hair blew across her face; the moon was a huge platinum disc. In the end she said, "All right, I have a past. We all do, don't we? I was planning to tell you when I got to know you a little better. Honestly I was."

"Do you want to tell me now?"

"No. But I will. I wouldn't want you to find out later from someone else and think I'd kept secrets from you."

"Suddenly I have the feeling I'd rather not hear it."

She went on as if I hadn't spoken: she said, "I'm a New England girl, which you must have known from the way I speak. My family were good people, I was brought up in a comfortable home and educated to be the kind of milk-pale porcelain girl they use to decorate Bostonian drawing rooms, full of sweetness and charm and very breakable. But when I was seventeen my father was ruined by specie speculation and killed himself in the traditional way—he jumped off the roof of a hotel in Albany. My mother lost her mind and died within a year and I had no other family. A girl I had known in school took me in—her mother owned a resort hotel in the mountains—only it didn't take me very long to learn it was more than just a hotel."

Her voice trailed off. With a premonition, I didn't look at her. Sweating in the heat, I wiped my palms dry on my trousers.

"I said I was breakable," she breathed. "But I didn't

34

break, not really. That woman threatened to put me out if I wouldn't be 'friendly' to the men clients. At first it was just fireside conversation, being company for lonely men who said their wives didn't understand them. They only wanted someone to talk to, a hand to hold, a sympathetic ear. But some of them wanted more than that, of course, and it got tiresome fighting them off. One of them was a man who'd known my father— he was persistent and I suppose everybody heard me screaming at him to keep his hands off me. Then in the morning he was found at the bottom of the mountain with his head broken open. I suppose he must have fallen and hit his head; he was too drunk to walk straight when I last saw him, but everyone thought I had killed him. I didn't have the nerve left to stay and face being arrested and tried. I ran away. I let a man pick me up on the Boston Post Road because I had no money and there was nothing else to do. He was a gambler on the run from bad debts and we seemed to have a great deal in common, so we were married in New York and we came to San Diego on a clipper around the horn after George won enough passage money in a card game."

She took a deep breath, audibly, and jerked her head around to fix her wide stare on me. "Do you know why I've told you all this?"

I made no reply, and presently she said, "It was to show you I trust you, Edward."

I watched her. Her glance dropped away, her toe described small circles in the dust on the porch floor.

Finally I spoke. "You know, Abby, I think I'd like to know you for a long time."

"Yes—yes."

"Well, then," I said, and could think of nothing to add.

She lifted her head to watch me with that direct blue gaze of hers and abruptly said, in a voice loose at the edges, "If I get drunk tonight will you promise to take advantage of me?"

I nodded slowly, and she seemed to grow looser and smaller in her chair; she became splendidly at ease, casually changing until her lids drooped with a drowsy expression that showed her willingness to give frankly when it pleased her, when the touch of my hand on her flesh pleased her. I got to my feet and took her hands and lifted her out of her chair. "You're a lot of woman, Abby."

"Hold me."

I touched her cheek with my fingertips, and felt it all the way down to my toes. I kissed her, and she said in a whisper, "Do that again"; and I embraced her tightly and felt the tremors of her desire. Full of her woman-smell, I turned her inside, through the store into her bedroom.

There was no hesitancy, no embarrassed self-consciousness: as if it had all been written down in the book before either of us had been born. We disrobed each other with slow pleasure. There was a sweat-shine in the cleft between her breasts; her pale body was soft and warm. We fell on the narrow bed together, joined by the quick swell of lusty demand. I bit the lobe of her ear gently; and felt her shiver, a shudder that passed along the length of her body. I kissed her, tasted the delicious soft warmth of her tongue. Her belly arched into me and she made small sounds in her throat, glutted with passion. Her breast came hot and swollen into my hand. I plunged into her throbbing, velvet, feminine snugness.

... The dawn was full with her pleasure. I tickled her ear with a finger and stopped her throaty laugh with a kiss, and lay back to explore the wonders of her body with my eyes. I said, "You are the promise I made to myself when I was fourteen years old."

"Don't tell me I'm the first, Edward."

"I didn't."

"How many others have there been?"

I closed my eyes smugly. "I couldn't begin to count."

"How many times have you been in love, then?"

"Hundreds. Thousands."

"You bastard."

"Once," I said. "With a sutler's niece in Florida."

"What happened?"

"She married a cattle farmer." I turned my head and opened my eyes. "You're very lovely in the morning."

"You're even uglier than I thought you were. But it's all right. I like you ugly."

"That's good. There ought to be some consolation for the fate worse than death."

She said, quite seriously, "I can think of no fate worse than death."

I extended my hand. "Shake on that."

"Shaking hands is for men." She rolled over and kissed me.

I emerged from the store in a tranquil state of mind that was soon shattered. The four pallets in the wagon shed were empty. There was no sign of my soldiers.

Juan Largo was tramping around the corrals when I came out. He shouted at me and I waited for him to come up. His long face was fiery. "You send them out on patrol by themselves?"

"No."

"Then I'm to take it they've gone off on their own?"

"You know as much as I do," I admitted.

"In which case," he said, "you owe me the price of three good wagon mules, Lieutenant."

"Three?"

"That's how many are missing."

Puzzled, I said absently, "You'll have to take it up with Major Heintzelman."

"Like hell I will," he began, and looked up past my shoulder. I turned to follow the direction of his glance, and saw Trooper Betts walking up the road from the trees that sheltered the Indian mission village.

Betts came up and I said, "Where are the others?"

He didn't know what I was talking about, but after he had a look inside the wagon shed he came back outside and said, "That's that, then. They didn't come down to the Innun camp with me last night. I thought it was kinda strange but I didn't count on this."

I said, "They're gone for good."

. "I expect they are, Lieutenant." He smiled slightly and in that instant I knew he had known all about it, all along. What puzzled me was why he hadn't gone with them.

Juan Largo said, "I'll take the price of those mules out of your hide if I have to, Lieutenant."

"You won't get much value from that," I said. "I'll tell you what you do—put it in writing and I'll sign it in your behalf. Present it to the paymaster in San Diego next time you go in for supplies. You won't have any trouble."

Juan Largo grunted an oath and drifted away.

I turned to Betts. "You knew they had it planned for last night, didn't you?"

"Maybe."

"You could have gone with them."

"I ain't a mule thief, Lieutenant."

"And that's all that stopped you?"

"Well, sir, I sure as hell ain't going to walk out of here on foot and by myself."

"Then it looks as if we're stuck with each other, Betts."

"For a little while, anyway, sir."

A buckboard wagon came rutting down the road, two men on the seat and a third riding the off-horse. The wagon bed was filled with molasses kegs. It bounced in from the flats and Juan Largo came out to stand beside me. One of the young men on the wagon seat said, "You Lieutenant Murray?"

I confessed to it. The young man withdrew a folded letter from his tunic and passed it down to me. "Army fellow at Yuma Crossing asked me to pass it on to you."

Juan Largo said, "You gents light and stay a while. Too hot to travel by daylight. Come inside, eat, maybe we'll have a little game of cards, what do you say?"

"No, thanks, amigo. We're bound for the diggin's, gonna grubstake ourselves with this load of molasses and got to get there before it curdles."

Trooper Betts came in sight. "Got room for a passenger?"

I looked at him. He was wearing civilian clothes. He said, "I've got five or six dollars to spare for passage up the line, gents."

"Climb aboard," said the driver.

Betts was watching me. I said, "You're not going anywhere."

"You can try to stop me, Lieutenant, if you're a mind to. Then we go through the whole thing next time again, and ever' time a wagon comes through. I expect you'll get tired of it faster'n I will."

Taking my silence for an answer, he stepped toward

the buckboard. I opened my holster flap and withdrew the revolver. "Hold it, Betts."

He looked over his shoulder. "I left my gun inside, Lieutenant. Along with all the other Army issue gear. You going to shoot me in the back when I ain't armed?"

"The penalty for desertion," I answered. "Turn around and come away, now."

He squared off to face me. Juan Largo and the pilgrims watched with fearful fascination, their eyes fixed on my revolver. Trooper Betts said, "Lieutenant, your people rousted me out of a saloon in San Diego one night last fall when I was minding my own business like a free citizen. I didn't put up too much of a fight when they shanghaied me and I didn't mind free grub for a few months with the Army, but I did my fighting in the Seminole campaigns and I've got places to see and things to do. Now I know the rules and regulations as well as you do; there was a time I was a fair-to-middlin' barracks lawyer, and you couldn't exactly call what I'm doing desertion. Ain't no enemy here, ain't no battlefield. All right, I've spent a while sizing you up, sir, and I've been obliged to know you, and I got no hard feelings, and I am pretty damn sure you won't use that gun on me today."

He was right, and he knew it. Confident but not cocky, he climbed up onto the wagon seat, where the two young pilgrims squeezed over to make room for him. The driver kicked the brake off, touched his hat brim, and bawled the mules forward. The buckboard broke out of its tracks, lurched, and pitched away. I put my gun away in its holster and when Betts waved at me I waved back. The wagon bucked away.

Juan Largo started to talk but I ignored him. I went up to the store and sat down in the rocker to read Sweeny's letter. Abby stood in the doorway, from which she had witnessed the whole thing. She did not speak until I looked up, signifying I had finished reading the letter. Then she said, "That was a good thing you did."

"He had the guts to face me and do it like a man. I couldn't shoot the man."

"You could have stopped him with your hands."

"Maybe I couldn't have licked him in a fair fight."

She smiled gently. "You weren't afraid of that."

"I guess not. I guess what it boils down to is, he was right and the Army was wrong. They shouldn't have shanghaied those boys in the first place. That's not the way you do things."

She said, "That letter is from your friend?"

"From Sweeny, yes."

"It's bad news, I can tell it from your face."

"Bad enough," I said.

I hitched the two mules to the dray wagon and walked around testing the load; it had to be tied down right for the rough trail. My throbbing muscles ached: Juan Largo, with petty spite on account of his mules, had refused to help load the wagon or even lend the assistance of his hostlers.

Abby came along scowling. "How long will you be?"

"I don't know."

"You don't have to snap at me, Edward."

"I'm sorry," I said. "Look, I don't know how you persuaded Juan Largo, but thank you."

"It didn't cost me. It doesn't matter."

"You didn't have to go out of your way to talk him into taking my Army chits."

She picked up a straw and made a great show of studying it as if it held some spectacular fascination. "He's scared of me, that's all," she muttered. "He can't afford to make me angry—if I left he'd have to run the store himself."

"Uh-hunh."

She looked up at me. "If I hadn't talked him into letting you have the wagon and things, would you have gone anyway?"

". . . Yes."

"That's what I thought. So you see it wasn't important. If I could have kept you here by telling him not to give you the supplies, I'd have done it."

I took both her hands in mine. "We haven't had much time, you and me."

"Enough to make me wish there was more." She leaned forward and kissed me. "That's to make sure you won't forget me."

"I've got a poor memory."

She laughed and kissed me again. But when I gathered the reins and climbed up to the wagon seat, her face was clouded. I said, "Abigail, I don't *want* to go out to Yuma, you know."

"I know. I read his letter. He's desperate and he's your friend. But I thought you had orders to stay here. Did that change when your soldiers deserted?"

"My orders were to protect travelers and not go more than ten miles west of here. I'm not going west, I'm going east, and any travelers that need protecting will be out there at the Crossing, not here. Besides, an officer in the field in the absence of his commander has pretty wide discretion in interpreting his orders. I know my military booklaw, you see. I expect the Major doesn't, but that's his lookout."

She pretended she was listening, but her face showed the deceit of it. She reached up for my hand.

"How long, Edward?"

"If he needs help I'll have to stay until this mess

gets straightened out. His men are the same kind I had here—if they go over the hill, he's got nothing between him and four hundred Indians but a revolver and a twelve-pound brass cannon."

"Edward, I—I won't tell you to be careful."

"You don't have to," I said, and lifted the reins.

THREE

From the high wagon seat I could see across the Colorado and up the Gila quite a distance, and I could not see a single leaf of green beyond the riverbank, nor a blade of grass, nor a thing that was not withered into the total drab brown-yellow of the desert.

It took me a while to find Pascual's village with my eyes; it was clay of the earth and the thatch was no different from the brush in the surrounding bottoms. Above, on the bluff, sunlight struck the polished brass cannon and the stubborn square outline of the stockade. I gauged the broken country between, the flayed landscape of rock and sand; my thoughts came sluggishly around to the wagon mules. They wanted very much to haul-ass down to the river, which they could smell—that ugly sun-splattered swirl of mud-brown turgidity and quicksand bottom. I kept my foot on the brake handle. It was too hot, and I was too exhausted to unhitch the team, and if I let them drag the wagon all the way down there, they'd never get it all the way up Sweeny's hill. It was a good two-hundred-foot climb to the top, where the bluff crested at the top of a cliff, commanding the river's elbow-bend. The top was flat, the cliff gave protection and command, and the Yuma villages were within half-mile cannon range. We had spent two days convincing the Dutchman it was a better site than the riverbank ferry-landing where the Dutchman had wanted to build.

The ferry sat heavy over at the Arizona side of the river, tended by a large brown-bearded tough whose naked chest glistened. The ferry's guy ropes sagged at midstream, bowing downriver with the current where it ran hard across the shallows. I remembered vividly the Dutchman's fuzzy-headed argument that we ought to move the whole shooting match—ferry, fort, and all—twenty miles downriver to Pilot Knob, to put distance between himself and the savages. Unhappily the wide Yuma bend, which slowed the current, made for the only practicable ferry-crossing between the Gila and the mouth of the Colorado, far down on the Gulf.

Where the ropes emerged at the near bank, in heavy thickets of arrow weed and stunt-willows, I saw an Indian lying in the shade. Not once did his head turn toward me. Maybe, in the heat, it would have required too much effort; maybe the river's lapping racket kept him from hearing my approach. But I had no trouble recognizing him—Caballo-en-Pelo, the lean Yuma war chief. He wore a calico breechclout, an Army officer's plumed cap, and a crimson string around the back of his head that supported his eye-patch. He had lost an eye in battle with the Maricopas two or three years before, when he had allegedly killed eleven enemy warriors. Now he was watching the ferryboat with the patient stillness of a predatory cat. I felt an uneasy shudder of premonition.

The wagon mules tugged and I talked to them in my polite, reasoning drawl: "To hell with goddamned you."

I kicked off the brake and sawed toward the slope that pushed uphill at Sweeny's little kingdom.

The rise looped up, steadily steeper; judging it, I began to doubt we would make it. The team and I had spent ourselves ploughing through the dunes, three days to make the last sixteen miles.

The sentry in the cannon tower gave the alarm; half-a-dozen soldiers exploded from the gate at a shuffling run. They were happy to see me: Corporal Crossthwaite, streaming sweat, bawled above the din, "Top of the fuckin' afternoon to you, Lieutenant!" They swarmed all over the wagon in their enthusiasm, bringing us to a lurching halt.

I had to bellow to make myself heard. "Goddamn it, get down off here and put your shoulders to it!"

Crossthwaite's crimson face was covered with dust and insect bites, ugly with sores; I had a close glimpse of that, and then he jumped off, roaring at the others. I got down, keeping the reins, and walked alongside the wagon to add my weight to the effort. The wagon creaked uphill. There was a lot of hoarse talk around me and I had trouble sorting it out. Someone in the tower fired off the cannon, a blank round; the boom was earsplitting. My head rocked back and I said, "What the hell was that for?"

"Summon Mister Sweeny," Crossthwaite replied.

I yelled at him: "Where is he?"

"Down making politics with them motherfucking Indians."

I didn't like his tone and I didn't like the way he had called Sweeny "Mister." It was an archaism you used only toward an officer you scorned.

I recognized Magruder and Bean among the weltering faces. They looked sick; feeble and flaccid. The wagon strained upward across rocks, men leaning to it under the lash of Crossthwaite's voice: "Heave, god-damn you lazy bastards." Bean almost caught his foot under the wheel; he jumped and yelped. The game mules scrabbled and in the end we crawled over the top, only just making it. Down below, I glimpsed an audience, a dozen Indians watching from the bottoms. We rolled inside the stockade and the sentry came down whooping and closed the gate, which made me scowl—the gate had always been left open when the regiment had been here.

The troopers sagged, beaten by the brief exertion. I couldn't remember seeing men so broken, even on battlegrounds in Mexico. They hung to the sides of the wagon, half-dressed and slack-mouthed, poking through the load with brief cries of happy discovery. I drew Crossthwaite aside: "What the hell's wrong?"

He gave me a bleak, unsteady glance. His eyes seemed glazed. "Been kind of rough out here, Lieuten-ant." He spun toward the sentry and bawled at him: "Charlie, goddamn it, get back up on that gun and reload it."

The trooper blinked and limped toward the ladder. Crossthwaite scraped the back of his hand across his mouth. "Been rough, Lieutenant. Rough."

"You said that."

"Did I? Yair, I reckon I did."

"What's the matter?"

He stared at his boots and licked his cracked lips. "Thanks for bringin' the food, Lieutenant. Gonna look like Christmas."

I watched him in disbelief. Crossthwaite was built like a truck horse, with vast shoulders and several chins. He looked as if he had been whipped beyond endurance. My attention shifted to the others—most of them had collapsed asprawl in the shade of the wagon. Dan Magruder, who had been the fightingest man in the regiment, came around the tailgate, stumbled once and caught his footing sluggishly, his eyes were dull with disinterest. Mullins and Ogle, Crouch, McCluan—odd I recalled their names, most of them hadn't been in my company or Sweeny's. They all had the look of men who had been chained for a thousand years to a burning rock in hell.

I said gently, "Let's get the mules unhitched and cared for."

Corporal Crossthwaite jerked as if I had struck him a blow. He mumbled, "I'm sorry, Lieutenant. I just forgot."

"Doesn't matter. Do it now."

"Yes, sir. Thank you, sir." He bawled names at three men: they got listlessly to their feet. They unhitched the team slowly, as if their hands were numb.

I said, "They'll want watering and rubbing down. Don't feed them too much."

Crossthwaite stirred with great effort and pointed toward what had once been officer's row. "Mister Sweeny's using the first tent there, sir. Take one of the others for yourself. Better beat the place for scorpions and snakes before you settle in."

A retort jumped to my lips but I stilled it. It was Crossthwaite's job to send a man into the tent and sweep it out, but they all looked so vulnerable that I said nothing. I took down my blanket-roll and duffel, shouldered them, and tramped toward the row.

I ducked into a tent, smashed a centipede under my bootheel and kicked it out through the open flap. I unfolded the canvas cot, set my things on it, and sat down on the edge of it, aches sprawling through all my muscles.

When I looked up, Crossthwaite was standing just

outside the opening. "I told them they could open a box of dates, sir. They need it. I hope you don't mind."

"It's all right, Crossthwaite."

His eyes were raw—he kept squinting and blinking as if he had a nervous tic, or grit under the lids. The hot, close air in the tent was like coarse wool, hard to breathe. I couldn't stand the heat; I got up and stepped outside. The setting sun fanned gray and pink across the clouds, and Crossthwaite turned to look past me at Sweeny's tent. He tensed up, and I turned to look that way.

An Indian girl had come out of the tent. She turned and gave me a direct look.

Crossthwaite growled in his throat. The girl gave him a little smile; she seemed at ease, there was nothing furtive in her manner. She was very small, dark and sultry, almost child-sized; yet full and ripe, with unclad nubile breasts and a nice round little ass. I must have tugged my breath sharply at the sight of her exposed body: it made her smile—a curious, incomplete smile that began but did not finish. It gave her a shy and charming appearance. She stared at me for a long interval before she turned and went away, walking with grace and pride; she seemed almost mystically serene. I watched her buttocks as she walked, until she turned out of sight past Sweeny's tent, whereupon I shifted toward Crossthwaite with a question in my eyes.

"She goes by the name of Rose," he said. "Or at least that's what he calls her. She's Mister Sweeny's cunt. If you'll pardon the expression, sir." His big-nosed face was closed up tight with disapproval.

"She's a Yuma?"

"Chief Pascual's granddaughter, I reckon."

I blinked, still astonished. "I never knew there were

any beautiful Indian princesses outside of Fenimore Cooper storybooks."

Crossthwaite picked at his scalp and studied his fingernail. "You likely saved our hides, sir, and we all obliged."

He was changing the subject and making no secret of it. I said, "Look here, Crossthwaite, just what in hell is going on here?"

"I guess you better take that up with Mister Sweeny, sir. Ain't my place to be talkin' out of turn." He drew himself up feebly, saluted, and dragged himself away.

I sat down inside the tent and scowled with baffled anger. It was as if I had entered an unreal realm through the garrison gate; nothing inside seemed quite in tune. Crossthwaite's evident displeasure all seemed to center around Sweeny—yet Sweeny had been the best-loved officer in the regiment. I had learned to discount the disgruntled mutterings of petty subordinates who complained of their superiors: it was natural for a man to resent anyone who was above him in the pecking order. Gripes easily became grievances; injustices became imaginary, resentments magnified reality, gossip became rumor. But these men weren't suffering from imaginary sickness, they weren't feigning hopelessness. The very air seemed thick with a sour heat, like the bitter smell that came from dying men's mouths on fields of battle. In my present exhaustion I was not prepared to make fine distinctions among tones of voice, but I was certain Crossthwaite's attitude toward Sweeny was one of grim and vivid hatred. A very personal thing. It was one thing to hate the Army, or this place, or the miserable condition of their lives; it was another thing entirely to despise Tom Sweeny with the unmistakable rage Crossthwaite had allowed me to glimpse.

...I heard a sentry's call at the gate and left my tent, emerging from Officer's Row onto the edge of the parade ground in time to see Sweeny march in through the gateway, accompanied by Troopers Knorth and Simmons. Knorth was bareheaded, shuffling at a foot-dragging gait; and I saw with amazement that his head had been shaved and he was dragging a small ball-and-chain on one ankle. I had seen that form of punishment in the regiment but I had never ordered it among my men, nor had Sweeny.

Sweeny came forward at a steady pace, his expression hidden behind thick hirsute underbrush. No one spoke to him. That was odd: someone, in the ordinary course of things, should have rushed to him with the news I was here with the supply wagon. But the men only stood, more or less at attention, watching him with fever-bright stares; not a word was spoken. I stepped forward and waved down the length of the parade ground, but it was not clear whether he had seen me in the waning twilight. He stopped by the buckboard and looked inside it, walked all the way around it, stopped, braced his feet wide, and yelled. "Corporal Crossthwaite. Front. And. Center."

Crossthwaite appeared beyond a row of tents and tramped forward, insolently slow. He drew himself up and made a precise salute, fingertips quivering, standing stiffly erect. I watched in mute amazement. Sweeny said: "What are you saving that button for? Button it up or cut it off. Pull in your gut and stand up straight."

Crossthwaite threw his shoulders back. Sweeny took the pipe from his belt and held it cupped in his palm. He said sharply, "How long has that wagon been here?"

"Maybe twenty minutes, sir."

"Then why isn't it unloaded?"

"Be cooler doing that heavy work after dark, sir."

"Do it now. Get everything under cover."

Without waiting a reply, Sweeny swung past him and came toward me. It was immediately evident that he had seen me, had known all along that I was there. A moment ago I had been ready to pummel him with the boisterous greetings of reunion; now, numbed and chilled, I stood carefully still and watched with narrowed eyes. When he approached I curbed my tongue and waited for him to set the tone.

He smiled, but it was fleeting. There were deep vertical lines between his eyebrows. "Ed," he said. "Ed." He shot out his hand and gently touched my arm with his pipe as if to reassure himself I was really there.

I felt awkward: confused, and embarrassed by my confusion. "Hello, Tom."

"Faith and begorra." He breathed, smiling again. "I am happy." But there was no joy in his voice.

"Tom——"

"Inside," he said, very softly.

The Indian girl, Rose, appeared without sound at the side of Sweeny's tent. Her eyes frankly coveted Sweeny; they shone when she looked upon him as they had not shone before.

Sweeny said something in Spanish, too rapid for me to follow, and the girl turned away without a word and faded into the shadows.

Sweeny turned past me and bent to go inside the tent. "Come on, Ed."

Crossthwaite was growling orders at the men. I ducked under Sweeny's tent flap. He was holding a sulphur match to a whale lamp. He settled the chimney and adjusted the flame, removed the pistols from his belt one at a time and dropped them on his camp table; gave me a sidewise glance and indicated a chair with

53

an offhand wave. It had been the Dutchman's camp chair.

I sat down talking. "All of you look like the wrath of God. In Christ's name, Tom—what's happened out here?"

"In Christ's name," he muttered. His voice was strange—as thick as if he had been drinking. But there was no odor of whisky. He said, "Christ himself was far better off than I am, I promise you. He had twelve followers and only one of them was a traitor."

"But what is it?" I was almost pleading.

He laughed off-key. "What is it? I'll tell you what it is, dear Edward. A snake or lizard that spends more than a few minutes in the noon sun here will fry to death like bacon in a pan."

That explained nothing. I knew it, and he knew I knew. He stirred and said, "Our red friends, of course— we could get our asses handed to us any time, we live with that every moment of every day, and no one can go on living under that forever. I haven't even troubled to count their strength, the many times I've been down to the village. What difference would it make? Whatever it is, we're obliged to take it on."

I felt my face color under his stare: I said, "Tom. These men are *sick*."

He nodded. Under the beard he seemed unnaturally pale. He spoke a word, spitting it out as if it were an insect that had flown into his mouth:

"Scurvy."

He jammed the pipe into the corner of his mouth. The veins stood out dark on the back of his hand. I said, "It can't be!"

"Believe what you want."

"I believe what I can, Tom."

His laugh was metallic. "It's bad food that does it. All salt provisions and nothing fresh out of the ground."

I swallowed. "But—*scurvy?*"

"Scurvy," he said in a dead, flat monotone. "We planted a vegetable garden but it wouldn't take; this ground up here's fit for nothing but weeds, you see."

"What about the bottoms?"

"Flooded out. Anyhow if we put a crop in down there the Yumas would steal it one night. There aren't enough of us, God knows, to go posting a guard on a vegetable patch."

A roar of booming sound rocketed across the garrison—someone had discharged the cannon.

I shot to my feet.

Sweeny said, "Sit down, it's nothing. We blow it off every night at the fall of dark. It has some small effect on the nerves of our copper-colored neighbors."

I settled into the chair very slowly. "It's all damn hard to believe, Tom."

"My good friend," he murmured, "if the appearance is bad, you must take my word for it, the reality is even worse."

He went on, curiously abstracted; he might have been talking to himself: "I've been annoyed to death by immigrants. They come across the river and seem to think I was left here for the sole purpose of attending to their wants. They help themselves to our private stores without a by-your-leave. So that, of course, there are now no private stores left. It's been weeks, you know. I took them out foraging—we turned up a few handfuls of wild onions and a little watercress upriver. I mixed a concoction from that and cactus juice and whisky for an anti-scorbutic—the whisky to mask the vegetables, otherwise we'd have gagged on it. Fresh greens will fight the scurvy, nothing else will do it. But

55

outside these gates we're pathetically easy targets and it gets harder every day to force any of these men to go outside with me. God, if you only knew—I've got such a goddamned bellyful of soloists who can't harmonize. I wish I had the strength to show you how glad I am you've come. You'll stay, won't you? Lord Jesus. I need your shoulders to carry part of this load."

The distance between us became stuffed with an awkward, padded silence. Finally I broke it: "Haven't any of them tried to go over the hill?"

"Knorth tried it."

"And that's why his head's shaved and he's trailing a ball and chain?"

"That's why," he answered evenly, meeting my eyes. "You have to watch them close, every minute."

"I'm not surprised. My four bravos deserted."

"These won't," he said. "The only way any of them will get out of here is in a box."

"That's strong talk, Tom."

"Cut tough meat and you need a sharp knife."

I made no response. Sweeny squeezed his eyes with thumb and forefinger, picked up his pipe and began to pack it. "And speaking of food," he added in a forced attempt at lighter tone, "I'm hungry enough to eat a horse."

He left his pipe behind; we went outside. The wagon stood empty against the far side of the stockade. Crossthwaite and eight of the men stood around a cook-fire on the edge of the parade ground; the ninth man stood guard in the tower. The pitiful loneliness of the scene struck me forcibly—the twelve of us, rattling around inside this regiment-sized fort.

Some of the crouching men struggled toward their feet. When Sweeny said nothing, I called forward:

"As you were."

They sank back with relief. I caught a few hopeful glances turning my way. None of them looked at Sweeny at all, except out of the corners of their vision.

Crossthwaite came away from the fire and met us out of earshot of the men. Sweeny said, "We'll be wanting something to eat too, Corporal."

"Then the squaw ain't cookin' tonight for you, sir?"

"Not tonight. And I'll thank you not to use that word again in my hearing."

"Word, sir?" Crossthwaite's innocence was crude and insolent. It made me bridle.

Sweeny said, in a very even voice, "Squaw, Corporal. Let me remind you, as long as the lady chooses to share our company we're not quite so likely to be eaten for breakfast by our friends down the hill. You'll treat her with every courtesy you'd afford a white woman."

"Sir, you mean——"

"Are you going to give me an argument, Corporal?"

"Do you want one, sir?"

Sweeny took a breath to steady himself. "You're out of line."

"Yes, sir."

"Have our meal brought to my tent."

"Yes, sir." Crossthwaite saluted and began to turn away.

"One more thing, Corporal."

"Sir."

"I assume you put the supplies in one of the tents?"

"In the old mess tent, sir."

"Post a guard on it," Sweeny said. "In the morning there'll be a job for all of you. I want all usable lumber gathered up from the compound. Knock down a few corrals and take apart the noncommissioned officers' privy, bust up anything else you can find except the stockade itself. Then knock out the north wall of the ammunition storehouse and build an addition on it, big enough to accommodate the supplies from Lieutenant Murray's wagon. You understand?"

"I understand, sir."

"I want it built tight, Corporal. You'll find a hasp and padlock on my footlocker. Remove them carefully and bolt the hasp onto the storehouse door. This time we won't have our stores raided—not by immigrants, not by Indians, and not by troopers. There's to be a guard posted on the storehouse at all times and I'll retain the key to the padlock. Have you got it all clear?"

"Clear, sir," Crossthwaite said, glacially.

Walking back to the tent, Sweeny said to me, "I'll let them eat their fill tonight and tomorrow. After that we'll have to ration the food. In case you wondered why it has to be locked up."

We went inside. Huge gray moths rustled around the lantern. I said, "Whatever happened to the old times, Tom—the good times, the laughing?"

"Too hot here to laugh." But he smiled. "Once in a while, though—last week I tried to describe ice to old Pascual. Ice. He didn't believe a word of it."

I chuckled; he didn't. He chewed his pipestem, brooding toward the fluttering moths. Crossthwaite brought food into the tent and left stiffly; it occurred to me I hadn't seen any of the men except Crossthwaite approach within talking distance of Sweeny. We ate in silence. I watched the way Sweeny consumed his food—deliberately, his jaw muscles bulging rhythmically. He took his time eating. "It's a joy to savor the taste of unsalted food," he said.

"You've changed, Tom."

"Have I? All right."

I thought he had meant to kill the subject, but a moment later he revived it. "The choice seems to be between changing and dying. There's only one thing left to us out here—staying alive. Nothing else matters much, everything but survival has to go by the boards. Don't judge me too quickly, Edward."

He spoke to me as if I were a stranger. Being with him was a strain: the old closeness seemed all gone, evaporated.

After he pushed his plate away he said, "I've been afraid to ask this, but I've got to. Can you stay?"

"Yes."

He slumped back in his seat. "You can't know how much that means to me."

"Did you expect anything less, Tom?"

"I never know what to expect, anymore," he said. "I've learned it's impossible to trust a lot of things I used to take for granted. Loyalty, the chain of command—it's all collapsed out here. I used to think I was a fair soldier—my men used to follow me."

"Maybe these will too, if you give them a chance."

He only shook his head dismally. "You just don't know, Ed," he breathed.

I stood up with great effort. "Maybe we'll get it all sorted out tomorrow, Tom. Right now I'm too damn whipped."

"Good night, then."

I left him sitting alone by the lamp; I went outside and walked along the row to my tent. Crossthwaite was there, emerging from the tent. He saluted and spoke:

"Brought you a basin and pitcher, sir."

"Why, thanks, Corporal."

He scratched a sore on his big nose. "You bringin' the wagon saved our skins, sir. The Major send you?"

"No," I said. "He didn't."

Crossthwaite's eyes widened briefly like those of a

weary marathon gambler when it dawns on him his opponent isn't bluffing, but does in fact have the good cards he represents. "You staying on, then, sir?"

"As long as I can, Corporal."

Reserving judgment, he only nodded and said good night, and drifted away. Quite clearly the world was divided into those who were for Sweeny and those who were against him, and Crossthwaite intended to wait and see which I was.

I was just turning to enter my tent when a shadow moved close to Sweeny's tent. I stopped and looked. It was Rose, the girl. She spoke softly and Sweeny appeared in the triangular opening, bent over, holding back the flap. Unaware that they were being observed, they stood together talking in Spanish, a word or two of which I picked up. The girl smiled at everything Sweeny said; her face, by indirect lamplight, was soft and compassionate. Sweeny casually rested a proprietary hand on her rump. After a moment they went inside his tent, and I retired into mine, ashamed of my eavesdropping. I remembered I hadn't asked Sweeny about the Indian girl. There were, in fact, a great many obvious questions I hadn't asked; my weary mind seemed to have slipped the track. I would clear it all up in the morning, surely. But just the same I was troubled. Back in New York, Sweeny had a girl, Ellen— his fiancée—he had always spoken of her reverentially. *Bird in hand,* I thought with drowsy irony; surely there was more than politics in the way his eyes had met the Indian girl's.

I stripped and settled on the cot, worrying it all around in my head; this place seemed so full of grim mysteries—and sleep struck me like a club.

FOUR

After reveille and morning mess Crossthwaite gathered the troopers around him and gave instructions. It did not escape my notice that the soldiers nudged each other when Sweeny came in sight—or that whenever there was something that had to be said to Sweeny, the message was taken to him by Crossthwaite. None of the others ever spoke voluntarily to Sweeny.

Crossthwaite parceled out jobs and they separated to various points around the compound; shortly I began to hear the squeak and bang of work. Sweeny stood on the parade ground sweating in the dark pool of his own long morning shadow. I offered him a cigar from Juan Largo's stock but he declined it, lighting his pipe instead. I said, "Where do we really stand with the Yumas?"

"They have got us by the balls and most of them know it."

"Can't Pascual keep them tame?"

"As long as he lasts. I've got no illusions about that—I suggest you don't entertain them either. Caballo-en-Pelo and Santiago and Antonio and the rest of them would just as soon have our hides, in strips."

"Why?"

He gave me a dry look. "The twelve of us stand between them and getting their ferryboat back. It comes down to that."

"No. They must know even if they killed us and took the ferry back, they wouldn't keep it long. More of us would come—and next time they wouldn't get off easy."

"I've explained that a dozen times. I suppose Pascual accepts it but the rest of them believe only what they see, and they see white men running the ferry and only twelve of us up here, twelve men and a cannon. Caballo-en-Pelo honestly believes the regiment left because the Major was afraid of the Yumas."

"Then he's a fool."

"Not that simple," Sweeny said, disarmingly mild. "Caballo-en-Pelo has a logical mind. He sees obvious facts and draws obvious conclusions. The only time the tribe ever had a real set-to with a sizable white force was last year with Morehead's militia—and the Yumas chased Morehead right back to Sacramento."

"You can't chase an Army anywhere if it chooses not to run," I said. "He ought to be able to see that."

"What he sees," Sweeny replied, "is that this is the Indians' home, not the white men's. He knows that gives them an edge. And he knows whites are scared of Indians, on principle. The sum of it is, Caballo-en-Pelo thinks he holds all the cards except one—the one being old Pascual. Caballo-en-Pelo and I vie for the old man's ear and up to now I've kept Pascual's favor, but the night will come when Caballo-en-Pelo gets tired of the game and decides to end it by slipping a knife through Pascual's ribs."

"Suppose he does. Will the rest of them follow him?"

"Certainly. Caballo-en-Pelo's a living legend, they'd follow him into hell."

"Then what are we doing here, Tom?"

"Standing our ground," he said.

"But what for? God, you can't feel any loyal allegiance to the Dutchman after what he——"

"Heintzelman is a swine. Loyal allegiance? Hardly. But what do you think I should do? Run for it? Just pull out and leave Yaeger's boatmen and the pilgrims to their fate?"

"If you put it that way, no."

"Then you see I've got no choice at all," he said.

I studied him. "Tom," I said, "there's more to it than that."

"More? You want more? Then I'll give it to you." His eyes gleamed at me—with anger: perhaps with fevered madness. "The Dutchman is trying to destroy me," he breathed. "He's not going to do it, Ed. I'm a better man than he is and I mean to prove it."

"At whose expense?" I demanded; but he made no answer. A hairy tarantula spider waddled out from under the edge of the empty tent beside us. It scuttled sideways, like a crab, along the band of shade. It was a good six inches across, gray and thick and balefully poisonous. Sweeny watched it for a while before he put his pipe in his teeth, threw his forage cap down over the spider and jumped on the cap with his bootheel. Then he flipped the shako over and scraped the remains out of the crown with his knife.

I said, "All right, Tom. You got plundered of your stores by pilgrims, the Dutchman didn't send the supplies he promised you, and you all took sick. You've got Caballo-en-Pelo hanging over you like a knife ready to stab. But something else has happened out here since the regiment left. There's a lot of hate spinning around this place; I can taste it, and it's a good deal more definite and personal than any of this can account for.

63

These men act as if they've got a grievance and I want to know what it is."

"It doesn't matter." He picked up his cap, inspected it with care, and settled it low over his eyes.

"Don't back away from it, Tom. There's nobody else you can talk to—either you let it fester inside or you tell me."

He made a face, sour. "Look, Ed, the Dutchman picked through every company in the regiment for the dregs to leave behind with me—and it didn't make any of these boys happy to know they were regarded as the worst men in the regiment. Except for Crossthwaite I've got nothing here but shanghai conscripts. And Crossthwaite came out of the guardhouse on Heintzelman's orders. A grievance? They hate my guts—because I've done my all-out best to keep them alive."

I wasn't satisfied with that; I opened my mouth to speak again, but the tower sentinel's voice rang across the parade ground, summoning the guard. Instantly both of us wheeled, on the run, ramming toward the gate.

The troopers assembled. Half had armed themselves; the rest carried hammers and pry bars. Crossthwaite, who had been nearest the gate, had gone swarming up the ladder to find out what was wrong; now he came down in a hurry and spoke to Sweeny in a fast, hard rasp.

"Thirty or forty men out there on horseback. They want us to open up."

"White men?"

"Yes, sir, but I don't like the look of them."

Sweeny went to the gate and peered one-eyed through a crack; when he turned to me he said dryly, "The Forty Thieves. Take a look."

I squinted through the crack. They were bunched in

a ragged group, a wild and filthy crowd, well mounted and festooned with pistols and caplock rifles. I heard Sweeny remark behind me, "About as desperate-looking a troop as ever broke the sixth and eighth commandments."

The bunch sat horseback only a few yards beyond the gate; the leader, a huge man in buckskins with a swarthy brigand's face, was shouting up toward the tower sentry: "Get that fucking gate open before we bust it down!"

Sweeny talked to the soldiers behind me with icy calm: "Magruder, Simmons, on me. The rest of you take rifle posts on the stockade. Get your weapons—on the run, now. When you get up there, keep cover but let them see your rifles. Lieutenant Murray, on the cannon."

I turned toward the ladder. Going past Sweeny I said in a low voice, "You're going out there?"

"Find out what they want."

"Better to talk to them from the tower, Tom."

"Not in my judgment," he said. "Go on up, Ed—use the gun if it comes to it." He swung toward the gate. Magruder and Simmons fixed themselves to him without a word.

I bounded up the ladder and reached the back of the tower platform, concealed from the Forty Thieves by the parapet; I swung toward Bean, the sentry, and spoke low:

"This thing ready to fire?"

"Yes, sir—loaded and clean."

I bent double and crabbed forward to the parapet, placed my hand on the gun-port wooden cover, and motioned to Bean to post himself behind the gun. "Light your fuse, soldier."

Bean licked dry lips and fumbled the lid off the fuse

keg. When he lifted the slow-match coil out he almost dropped it. He held a trembling sulphur match to the end of the three-foot fuse and held the sizzling coil ready in his right hand. It would smolder half an hour or so before needing replacement.

I depressed the muzzle of the cannon to the bottom of its arc and nodded to Bean. He put his shoulder to it, rolled it forward until the muzzle rammed the flap door. I yanked the door aside and Bean shoved the gun onto its wheel-chocks. The muzzle protruded six inches past the stockade, pointed downward now, into the midst of the mounted party. I turned back to the head of the ladder and caught Sweeny's eye. He had been waiting for my signal; now he nodded, spoke to Magruder and Simmons, and gestured to Crossthwaite, who slid the gate-bar back and made a narrow opening, through which Sweeny slipped like an eel. Magruder went through right behind him. There was a growl of voices from the Forty Thieves; Simmons, at the gate, hung back, and Crossthwaite shoved him forward through the opening, pushed the gate shut and slammed the bar into place.

The half-dozen remaining troopers had swarmed up the inner walls of the stockade to the parapet, where they crouched on rifle platforms and poked their rifles through the port cutouts. Inspecting their positions with one swift sweep of my glance, I gathered my legs under me and stood up beside the cannon, in plain sight of the mounted troop below.

Sweeny had walked forward to within seven or eight feet of the leader's horse. Magruder and Simmons were ranged behind him to either side, rifles at port arms and cocked; Sweeny had his hand on the revolver in his belt.

In time the hubbub of talk from the toughs died

down sufficiently for Sweeny to make himself heard. "Now what's this all about? What's *your* name?"

The brigand ignored the second question. "We need provisionin', soldier."

"You won't get it here."

The brigand's eyes expressed his contempt for the diminutive one-armed man on the ground before him. "Then I reckon we just gon bust a hole in your big old fort." His rifle was canted across his saddle pommel; now he lifted it in his right hand. The muzzle swung vaguely toward Sweeny and the brigand smiled thinly.

Sweeny said, "Your threats are wasted, friend. You're talking to the United States Army."

It elicited a laugh from the crowd; horses pushed forward and I heard the brittle snaps of rifle hammers drawing back to full cock. Sweeny spoke sharply:

"Take a look up there and count up the odds before you get notions."

I balanced my revolver casually across the parapet and saw their heads swivel upward, their eyes travel the length of the rifle-studded parapet and come to rest on the blunt barrel of the brass cannon.

Sweeny said, with considerable exaggeration, "One shot from that gun will blow half of you out of your saddles. You can sell your lives for provisions if you want, but I imagine you'll get more bullets than bread."

There was an angry rumble of low talk; I heard one of them say distinctly, "They's only ten, twelve of them, Floyd, the boatman wasn't lyin'. We can take 'em."

"You can try," Sweeny said flatly.

Trooper Simmons had backed up until his shoulder blades were hard against the gate; the rifle trembled in his grasp and Magruder gave him an over-the-shoulder glance of angry contempt. Floyd, the brigand, scraped the back of his hand across his mouth and squinted speculatively at the cannon, at me, and at the half-dozen rifles along the stockade. If he hadn't had an audience he probably would have given it up for a bad bluff, subsided, and turned away; but his crowd egged him on, and if he was their leader he was also their prisoner—if he backed down now he would lose their respect, and among these lawless ones it would probably mean he would soon be challenged for leadership and killed. Floyd was in a bind.

There was only one thing left for him to do, and I knew suddenly what it was; and so I wasn't surprised when Floyd growled abruptly, dropped his rifle, and launched himself bodily from the saddle in a heavy leap against Sweeny. Sweeny had the sense to roll with it; they went down in a tangle.

I shouted a warning down the line of troopers on the stockade: "Hold your fire."

The brigand had Sweeny outweighed by six or seven stone. They rolled clumsily in the dust, broke apart and clambered to their feet, hard-breathing, glaring at each other. Sweeny's face was a mask behind the black beard. Floyd was a study in disgust—a false front, I was sure, concealing fear. Fear, and the still greater fear of showing fear. For even while he knew he could whip Sweeny, he was terrified of what would come after.

Expecting the giant brigand to make short work of it, I wasn't prepared for the quick decisive reversal that followed. I should have remembered that Sweeny, who had come to America at the age of twelve, had spent his adolescent years in the tough back streets of Brooklyn.

Floyd circled in toward him, ready to grab, seeing before him a slim little man with only one arm. One squeeze of Floyd's big arms would make kindling of him.

But Sweeny wasn't ready to fight by Floyd's rules. He drew Floyd with him, back toward the log stockade until Floyd began to smile with the certainty he had Sweeny trapped against the wall. And then Sweeny bounced himself off the wall like a carnival acrobat, threw his legs in the air and slammed his bootheel brutally into the brigand's face.

Floyd went down hard. The ring of his awful howl echoed. Sweeny alighted neatly, surefooted; wheeled, snapped a grip on Floyd's flailing wrist, and broke Floyd's elbow across his own bent knee. The snap of it was loud and brittle. Sweeny's teeth formed an accidental smile. He braced the stump of his right arm against Floyd's chest, gripped Floyd's ear and twisted. Every one of us heard him clearly:

"Now tell them to get away from here or I'll rip your ear off."

Stunned to immobility, I watched with unblinking amazement. No one stirred; no one spoke. Floyd seemed only half-conscious; his legs thrashed weakly with pain but he made no response to Sweeny's command. Most likely he hadn't even heard it; his face was a cruel bleeding mess, his arm was bent unnaturally against his side.

I knew, in a dazed fashion, it was time to act. I broke out of stasis, lifted my revolver and cocked it crisply in the air. "All right." I had to clear my throat. "All right—don't get forward. Leave his horse and one man to care for him. The rest of you back away. *Move.*"

I waited until the crowd had reached the bottom and circled toward the riverbank. I spoke to Bean—"Stay put and mind this cannon"—and scrambled down the ladder. I let myself out through the gate and held my revolver cocked on Floyd's horseback companion while Sweeny released Floyd's ear and got to his feet.

Sweeny looked up at the man on horseback, who dismounted slowly, keeping his hands in plain sight. Sweeny said, "You'll want to splint his arm before you move him."

"Uh."

"Use his rifle," Sweeny told the man. "I don't think you people will want to try this again, will you?"

"Lieutenant," the tough muttered, "we've made all kand of mistakes in ahr tam, but we rarely make the same mistake twass."

"Your people will be choosing a new leader. Make sure he knows our cannon is always loaded."

"I reckon you won't be troubled by us again," the tough said stiffly.

"You're headed for the camps?"

"Naw. Been there. We was fixin' to move on into Mexico." There was a sudden, cruel smile: "Just as lief git ahr gold out of them *ranchos* as have to dig it out of the grand."

Sweeny said, "The whole bunch of you aren't worth the powder it would take to blow you to hell. You won't find the Mexicans as easy to trample as you think."

"Maybe—maybe. But I reckon it's as good a place to die as any." The tough picked up Floyd's rifle and placed it beside Floyd's broken arm, and began to rip Floyd's shirt into strips. Floyd himself had lost consciousness.

Sweeny said, "Get that out of here as soon as you can," turned, made a sweeping motion with his arm, and led the way inside through the gate.

The blood was still pumping in my veins; I was trembling when I helped Simmons lower the crossbar into place. Sweeny, a few paces ahead of us, wheeled suddenly and leveled a finger at Simmons.

"You," he snapped. "Front and center."

Simmons gave me the look of a startled rabbit, swallowed with a great heave of his Adam's apple, and hurried forward to stand at attention.

Sweeny said, "You'd have been useless out there if it had come to a fight."

How in hell had he had time to see that, I wondered.

He went on, using his voice like a fist: "If I have to shove a poker up your ass to give you a backbone then that's exactly what I'll do. Until further notice you will be water carrier for the detachment. By yourself. You'll carry slung rifle and side arm and you'll do the work of two men. Am I understood clearly, Trooper?"

Simmons' throat kept working; he only nodded, unable to speak. Sweeny turned away in contempt, and raised his voice: "Crossthwaite, get them back to work."

I followed Sweeny across the parade ground as far as the mess tent, where he paused under the canvas awning and dipped a cupful of water from the open keg. It was a ten-gallon barrel with twin handles. Ordinarily, water duty was a three-man duty—two men to carry the keg down to the river, fill it, and drag it up to the top of the bluff; the third man to carry the weapons of all three and maintain security.

I said, "That could be a mistake, putting him on water duty by himself. Never mind the discipline question—he'll make an inviting target."

"That's what I want," Sweeny said. He didn't bother to look at me.

"Things are bad enough without risking the loss of a man," I retorted. "We've only got ten of them to start with."

"He won't get hurt. The Indians aren't ready to start jumping us yet. They'll harass him a little—I hope it will toughen him up. It had better."

"You're taking a chance with his life, Tom."

He turned, then, and his eyes penetrated me like weapons. "I intend to take every chance, until there are no more chances left. It's no time for caution."

Sweeny left me there at the mess tent; he quartered across the corner of the parade ground toward his own tent. The Indian girl materialized from somewhere and met him at the flap, where the two of them stood talking softly. I swept the rest of the compound with my glance and found Crossthwaite standing not far away, sweating and watching Sweeny and the girl with an unfathomable expression. His flesh was red; he was a big-nosed brute, covered with sores. He stood with his head lowered, his left elbow cupped in his right palm and the fingernail of his left hand inserted thoughtfully in his nostril. When he caught me looking at him he dropped his hand away. I went to him, moving casually, and spoke with an air of amiable conspiracy:

"Sometimes he seems damn tough on the men, doesn't he?"

Crossthwaite's distrusting glance flicked across my face. He grunted a wordless reply.

I said, "He's upset by what happened just now. You'd be too. When he cools down I'll talk to him about it."

Animated by what I had said, Crossthwaite nodded quickly. "I hope you do that, Lieutenant. That hill gets mighty steep to climb when you got to haul all the water up from the river by yourself. And it's a damn high hill to climb in a lot of other ways too, if you get my meaning."

"Maybe you'd better spell it out for me."

He inspected his fingernail. "You're an officer, sir."
Meaning: officers stick together.

I said, "I'm the only one you can talk to about it,
Crossthwaite."

His big shoulders lifted and dropped. "Look, sir, I
tried to take Mister Sweeny's side. Honest to God I did.
I mean, we both fit in the Mex War, we both soldiers,
not like the rest of these conscripts we got here. But
you can't expect these kind of animals to behave like
line soldiers—and that's exactly what he does expect,
that much and a whole lot more, and when they don't
deliver it he jumps all over them, sick or not. Ain't a
man Jack in the detachment ain't been whipped at
least once. A man gets goddamn tired of being crapped
on, sir. You got to see the men's side of it—maybe
Mister Sweeny ought to try pretending the rest of us
are almost half as good as he is."

"Easy to say. You don't have to wear his hat."

"But he does," Crossthwaite said. "And I mind sometimes he don't wear his hat square on his head."

"Meaning?"

He changed his expression evasively. "Oh, I don't
know, sir. The heat gets to everbody now and again.
Maybe that Yuma squaw could turn a man's head."

"Turn his head and make him do what?"

"I wouldn't want to say, sir. I mean, it ain't nothing
but rumors among the men, you know."

"What sort of rumors?"

"Well, you got to see how they feel. It ain't exactly
reassurin' to feel maybe Mister Sweeny thinks more
of that squaw than he does of his own men. White men.
Some of them are real scared maybe one day he'll sell
the rest of us out for her sake. Give the Indians a crack
at the rest of us in return for them lettin' him marry
the squaw. It wouldn't be the first time that kinda

73

thing happened. You seen the way them two look at each other, Lieutenant? Makes a white man's skin crawl, I don't mind risin' to remark."

"I think you're underselling Lieutenant Sweeny, Corporal. He'll never sell his men out. Not for gold and not for any woman alive."

"Easy for *you* to say, sir," he said, insidiously echoing my own speech. "You ain't never had to make that kind of choice."

"If she tried to force him to make that kind of choice, she wouldn't be the woman for him. He knows that, Corporal."

"I knowed you'd take his side," he said with stubborn self-righteousness.

When the naked sun climbed high the men surrendered to it and took shelter. I went outside the gate and stood on the back of the bluff, looking toward the river. A plume of dust far out on the eastward desert was a sign of Floyd's party of brigands, filibustering their way toward Mexico, where I had no doubt a brutal fate awaited them, as it always would their kind. Sweeny had handled them superbly, and in so doing he had helped reassure me. He was still the same Sweeny who had fought with such cool precision at Cerro Gordo, where men had followed him eagerly into certain death not because of Army orders but because he was Fighting Tom Sweeny, laughing black Irishman, beloved comrade in arms, leader of men. Kearny himself had called him the best soldier in Mexico. One night in April of 'Forty-seven he had slept between the corpses of two dead Mexicans to keep warm, and in the morning his men had arisen out of the fields like ghosts to carry on the battle—not one had deserted in the night. He had fought the whole day like a pirate, although wounded in the thigh, until cannon shell exploded directly under him, tearing apart his good right arm. It had taken that much to bring him down. In the years since, I had become convinced nothing would ever bring him down again: he seemed invincible. But now the parts of him were stripping away. The laughter was gone; the high, careless ease, the loose indolence of our friendship, all gone.

Thinking back, I realized now how eagerly I had allowed his brutal victory over Floyd to reassure me—how easily I had let it convince me of what I wanted to believe. My mind had been made up about him for so many years that it was impossible not to resist changing my opinion; I saw now how dangerous, how likely, it would be for me to continue resisting the change even if proof should confront me, contradicting the past. Had Sweeny changed more than I wanted to admit? Was he now given to imperial caprice, whimsical brutality, as Crossthwaite insisted? His treatment of Floyd—it could as easily support one opinion as the other. And suddenly I was afraid, a knot of fear lumping in my belly—because I did not *know* Sweeny anymore.

FIVE

I stood on the back of the bluff watching the brigands' dust-cloud diminish toward Mexico; presently, in a state of uncertain fear and depression, I turned back toward the gate—and saw Caballo-en-Pelo standing silent and erect, watching me from fifty yards away. He carried an old .69-caliber trade musketoon in the crook of his elbow. His face was puckered with scars and creases, dominated by the crimson patch over his left eye.

I slowly lifted my empty palm. Caballo-en-Pelo was brown-skinned and lean, very tall as Yumas were. I repeated the sign of friendship but he only watched me, changeless. I stood rooted, feeling fear—not any immediate fear of what he might do now, but a creeping sense of slow doom. He was sizing me up with a slow appraisal, insolent by its very expressionlessness. To show him I wasn't impressed, I turned my shoulder to him coolly and walked toward the edge of the cliff, deliberately putting my back to him—knowing he would have to cock the musketoon if he planned to use it, and I would hear that in plenty of time.

But when I reached the precipice and turned to look back, Caballo-en-Pelo was gone.

It was as if by his wordless appearance and retirement he meant to convey a message to me: *Your time is short here, it is your last chance to escape.*

I watched Indians' shadows shift in the village below. The Yumas, in whose huts each day began with a recital of dreams, called themselves *Kuchiana,* Good People; they tilled the hard clay soil and went to war, as a rule, only as a casual diversion against the pestilential Yavapais who lived upriver and raided Yuma crops in good years. Old Pascual, like several of his predecessors, possessed a valued sheaf of certificates, obtained from travelers and attesting to the chief's good character—of these he was very proud. The ferryboat had supported them for centuries, since the first Spanish missionaries had laid out the chain of California missions. And now the ferry had been taken away from them. You didn't have to be a hand-wringing sentimentalist to see the injustice of it.

Below on the river, a boatman stood paying out rope as the ferry moved away from its dock with a high-sided freight wagon on board; and four Indians floated downstream on balsa rafts carrying small watermelons, all they had been able to salvage of the stunted-out crop from upriver fields. Old women with wattled breasts stood on the bank coiling grass ropes, ready to throw the lines to the raft polers and bring them to shore. All of them moved with slow lethargy; the malaise of the desert was epidemic. It lent a feeling of timelessness, of boredom, as if nothing could ever happen here, as if nothing would ever change. But the ghost of Caballo-en-Pelo stood in my vision like an afterglow—a white man's gun in his hands, with which to fight white men. *Why do they have to imitate us at our worst?*

Abby Marshall's image kept intruding; she had haunted my restless dreams all night, and now, thinking of her and looking down into the village, I found my thoughts coming around to Sweeny's Indian girl who, though she hadn't yet spoken a single word to me, had left me with an impression of clear-eyed compassionate wisdom. For reasons of her own (or of grandfather Pascual's?) she had offered herself as a free hostage; she was always close to Sweeny wherever he went. Only when he walked down to the Yuma village, in the middle of the afternoon, did she remain behind.

Sweeny was gone for several hours. During the afternoon, travelers piled up on the far side, waiting their turns, and came over on the ferry in steady waves. Some of them stopped at the garrison. They were drab mostly, and bored, with tired sunburned skin; they were anxious to unburden themselves of the horrors they had endured, and with deadly repetition they all told the same tales of waterless heat, wagon breakdowns, Indians sighted on horizons, chalk-white bones of animals and men on the trail, and of those who had died of heat and disease. They claimed a platform in our company for the expression of their complaints, as if our understanding could help at all; and finally they went on, leaving us, plodding away until distance absorbed them from sight. But before they left, several of them became belligerent when we did not roll out a red carpet to them. I had to explain our limitations at least four times in as many hours, and there were a few who refused to believe me:

"Where's your headquarters, soldier?"

"Right here."

"But where's the Army, then?"

"We are the Army, pilgrim."

"Come on, don't josh me!"

None of them had any supplies they were willing to give, or sell, to us. In any case they had no faith in Army scrip. This close to the gold country, paper of any nature was worthless. Crossthwaite confided in me,

"Been like that all the time we been here, sir. Always takes them two weeks longer than they planned to get this far, and they ain't got the fixin's left to feed themselves through the dunes, let alone spare any food for us."

Then he said, "I got to take a leak," and left me to deal with the pilgrims alone. Crossthwaite had always had a conveniently weak bladder.

Sweeny returned around five; the girl met him at the gate, but retired from sight when a wagon party of pilgrims came uphill to the garrison to beg supplies, which we had to decline by reciting a litany that had already become tiresome to me after only one day of it. One passenger aboard the wagon was a priest who said he was headed for the Gomorrah of the goldfields to save souls. There ensued a brief exchange between Sweeny and the padre that did nothing to soothe my increasing agitation over the explosive changes that seemed to have taken place in Sweeny's character. In his irreverent and erratic way Sweeny had always been devout, toward his Maker if not toward his Church; yet now, in response to the padre's friendly blessing, Sweeny snapped, "Don't be talking of God up here, Father."

"What's that?"

"God has turned his back on this place."

"Are you a Catholic, Lieutenant?"

"Yes. No—I don't know any more. Out here what difference does it make?"

"I think perhaps it is you, Lieutenant, who have turned your back on God. Remember you exist only because of His infinite wisdom."

"Out here, Padre, man exists in spite of God, not because of Him."

"That's perilously close to blasphemy."

"I've heard it called the land that God forgot, Padre. Look around you—and disagree with that if you can."

"We are all children of God," the priest said, squirming uncomfortably on the hard wagon seat.

"When it counts," Sweeny said, pressing the point out of all proportion to its weight, "God is never there."

"Perhaps I had better stay over and hear your confession, Lieutenant."

"No, Padre. Out here it is I who should hear God's confession. I feel I'd be up to it today—I feel inspired to it." There was a wicked gleam of fever in his eyes.

"Inspired," the priest murmured disapprovingly, "means to be touched by the hand of God. You're troubled, young fellow, and God understands that. *The Lord is my rock and my fortress*—don't turn your back on Him."

The wagon driver, impatient, lifted his reins and bawled at the team; the wagon broke into movement and gathered speed on the downhill slope. The priest was twisted on the seat, looking back; Sweeny lifted his canteen in a gesture of toast and muttered, "To the companions of God," and took a drink. The priest was still craned around looking at us, full of concern, and Sweeny said, "I hope to hell he doesn't decide to jump off the wagon and come back to save my soul."

"The Gospel According to Sweeny," I said, not smiling at all.

His eyes whipped around against me. "Pascual is losing his grip on them, Ed. Red men and white men—it looks like we'll soon be killing each other. So tell me this—which is the color of an immortal soul? Ask the priest about that, ask God about that. Which side do you suppose God is on, now?"

"Maybe we'd just better hope we are on God's side," I answered.

"But we aren't. That's just it."

I had no answer to that; he was dead right.

The heat of drought scorched and cracked the surface of the earth. Plants shriveled under the sun; men, streaming sweat, staggered at their work. But by sundown the reconstructed storehouse was pronounced sound by Sweeny, who hooked his padlock onto its door and banged it shut with a crisp finality that set my teeth on edge. All our food and powder was locked up inside—and Sweeny had the only key.

A hail from the sentinel sent us to the gate; we peered through and saw a slouch-seated horseman coming up the twilit grade, leading four pack mules. Sweeny said, "Praise be. It's Antoine, isn't it?"

"Damned if it isn't," I said. "Open the gate, Magruder."

Antoine Leroux rode into the compound with an agonized grin all over his seamed face. "H'are yew, folks?" He lifted one spindly leg over his saddle pommel and stepped down, spry and agile, reaching out to shake our hands. "Tom—Lieutenant. Glad to see y'all—them dunes drifted over some since last time I come acrosst, fuckin' hard going out there."

Sweeny greeted him with more warmth than I had seen him display any time recently; but it was forced, and dropped away from him quickly. He turned: "Four mule loads. That's all the Major sent."

"The Major didn't send nothing," Antoine growled. "Me and Hardcastle scared it up."

"Hardcastle must have got at least one of my letters, then?"

"Got tew'r three. When I left he was settin' up to see General Smith, take your letters along and show 'em to the general. Might take a little while, Army channels bein' as they are, but I reckon you gonna git some hep before too long now. Lieutenant, how come you to be here?"

I told him over supper. Rose came in from the shadows where she seemed to spend much of her time in Sweeny's absence; she seemed to know Antoine from before and exchanged casual conversation with him during the meal in Sweeny's tent. I was surprised by the quality of her Spanish. She spoke well; it wasn't the pidgin Spanish of the other Yumas. I wondered where she had learned it. From Sweeny? No, his own Spanish was poor compared with hers; besides, he would more likely have taught her English.

Her voice was rich and musical, quite low and throaty for such a small woman. I caught myself staring at the downed cleft between her sturdy breasts; I looked away, trembling at her ripeness, and found Sweeny watching me with his face stern. I colored and addressed myself to my meal.

The girl was talking animatedly to Leroux; I followed enough of the Spanish they spoke to realize she was a far more unusual girl than I had supposed. She had a keen mind and a sharp, if somewhat wry, sense of humor: Sweeny had mentioned the missionary priest and she was saying, "There were missionaries here for many years, Jesuits and after them Franciscans, but they didn't make many converts. They tried to teach us to hate ourselves—tried to tell us we weren't as good as they were. Like you Anglos—you call us noble." She smiled with a twinkle. "But you think we're simple children or crazy wild animals. You think the best Indian is the one who becomes most like you."

"If you mean me personally," Leroux said in Spanish, "I always thought the best white man was the one who

83

became most like an Indian. But then I'm part Indian myself."

Sweeny spoke suddenly: he leaned forward, intense. "Why is it we can't live together without hate?"

And the girl said, "Because your people spoil the land, they can't leave it alone. Give us back our ferryboat and we will live without hate—that is what Caballo-en-Pelo says."

"And what do you say?"

"Oh, but I was taken away by Spaniards as a child and lived ten years among them. Almost a slave, yes, but I learned a white man's language and reading, and I learned how the white man thinks, and when I came back I told the people what I'd seen. My grandfather believed what I told him. The others weren't wise enough—they believe what they want to believe, and they want to believe what Caballo-en-Pelo tells them."

I broke in: "The Spaniards took you to Mexico as a child?"

"Yes."

"But when you grew up you came back?"

"Yes."

"Why? To teach them the things you learned from the Spaniards in Mexico?"

"Not at all," she answered. "I don't think the Spaniards have anything to teach the people."

"Then why?"

Her answer was a wide-eyed look of surprise and a vague, almost shy, gesture. "Because I'm not a Spaniard—I'm a Kuchiana. Would *you* rather live among the Spaniards than among your own people?"

"Now that you put it that way—no."

The girl turned toward Sweeny with a radiant smile of triumph. "Your friend," she said to him, "is another one of *them*. He can't believe an Indian who has seen the white man's way of life could possibly choose the Indian way." But, strangely, she was laughing at me. She thought it was amusing. I began to regard her with considerable awe.

I said, "It seems to me you think like a white woman. Your sense of humor, for example——"

It made her eyes flash. She snapped at me, "Do you think no one but whites can laugh? What if I tell you I have cried helplessly with laughing from a joke performed by Caballo-en-Pelo? Do you know how the Kuchiana must restrain themselves to keep from whooping with laughing when you silly white warriors prance and strut back and forth in stupid straight lines, with one man yelling orders at the others and the other men all stepping at the same time with no more dignity than a line of red ants on the ground?" She was watching me earnestly; but now, the very thought made her giggle and she turned her face against Sweeny's shoulder. Leroux's face was creased into a pained grin; Sweeny looked wistfully amused but his eyes were faraway and bitter, he was thinking of something else.

I said stubbornly, "I still think you act like no other Indian woman I've seen. To speak up as you do in the company of men—is that the Indian way?"

"I can't speak for other tribes. Among the Kuchiana the women are much more free than the Spanish women in Mexico. We sit on all tribal councils except one—and that is because it is the men who make war." She grinned again—"Because they are good for nothing else. Not unlike yourselves, I think."

It made Antoine laugh; I had to smile too. "You're far more outspoken than most of the white women I know," I confessed, but naturally that made me think of Abby, who would be a match for this one, and whom I found myself missing with unexpected anguish.

We finished our supper; Rose gathered the utensils and left the tent, and the three of us went outside to enjoy what there was of the nightfall breeze. The men had two fires burning outside the mess tent; their shadows wavered in the dimness. Sweeny looked to the sky and murmured, "I've been dreaming of rain for months."

"Not likely 'fore September," said Antoine.

Sweeny reamed out his pipe and packed it. I said to him, "What an amazing creature she is."

"To be sure," he breathed, glancing toward the mess area, where the girl was bent over the trough scraping the plates with sand before rinsing them in the precious water of the shallow dishpan.

I said, "Imagine an Indian girl washing dishes."

"Well," Antoine observed, "it ain't as if they ain't had plenty to do with white folks, runnin' that fuckin' ferryboat two, three hundred years. These Yumas ain't exactly the same kand of folks as the pony-war Innuns you meet back on the prairie. Git as old as me, Lieutenant, you'll fand they's a lot more different kand of folks kickin' around this old earth than you knowed about when you stard out."

"That's all good and well, Antoine," said Sweeny in his beaten, weary voice, "but how does it keep us from killing each other off?"

"Beats shit out of me, Tom, but I be pissdamned if I want to see it commence."

I said with a straight face, "We could always massacre Yaeger and the boatmen and give the ferry back to Pascual."

"Times I'd rather do that than kill Yumas," Sweeny said. "Do you know I once seriously asked Yaeger to give it back to the Indians?"

"What did he say?"

"Said it wouldn't do any good. Some new bunch of

whites would come along and take it away from them again. And the damnable thing is, he was right. They may take it back but they'll never hold onto it. It just isn't in the cards."

"Rose knows that," I said. "Pascual knows it."

"Rose and Pascual aren't the ones we'll have to kill," he intoned dully, "and get killed by." Puffing his pipe, he turned half-around toward the tent, but then he stopped, his head snapping back, eyes going wide with instant rage. I wheeled to follow the direction of his gaze, and saw Magruder near the girl, by the dishpan. Evidently he had come to it with dirty mess plates and dumped them on the earth at the girl's feet, expecting her to wash them. I gathered easily enough from her stance that she had refused, and when my eye struck him Magruder was in the act of spitting on the ground and turning away in contempt.

The girl made no response; she only stacked her own plates, left Magruder's in the dirt, and turned toward us. But Sweeny walked past me, his boots tramping the earth emphatically; he walked right by the girl without turning his head and headed straight on toward the nearer campfire. I said to Antoine, "Come on," and we set out after him. The girl gave me a puzzled look but I only shook my head at her and went on with Antoine.

The men got sluggishly to their feet at Sweeny's approach. "Magruder," he barked. "Front and center."

Magruder came away from the fire and squared his shoulders, "Sir," he said—almost, but not quite, smartly. One corner of his lip was slightly curled.

I was right behind Sweeny; I moved close enough so that he would feel my weight behind him and I said under my breath, "Tom—drop it." He would be making a bad mistake if he made an issue of it; far better to have let it ride—but he committed himself to it:

"Prepare yourself for company punishment, Magruder. Corporal Crossthwaite—bring the lash."

Crossthwaite took two paces away from the fire and said with distinct animosity, "On what charge—sir?"

I couldn't remember ever having seen Sweeny truly angry before; now it chilled me, a bleak coldness that came off him like death. He spoke without animation in a hard, pitchless voice. "Disobedience of a direct order from the commanding officer. Every one of you has heard me plainly state that the lady is to be treated with every possible courtesy."

Crossthwaite trembled in anger. "Sir—Magruder didn't say a word to her."

"Who gave you permission to speak, Corporal? Get the lash!"

The two of them stood ten feet apart, staring at each other in a desperate contest of wills. Magruder, for the moment forgotten by them both, stood full of fury and venom—flesh aquiver, eyes bulging. Sweeny was like a statue, motionless and unblinking, staring Crossthwaite down. In an effort to break it up, I stirred and walked deliberately to a spot ten feet to Sweeny's left, hoping my movement would draw their eyes away from each other; Crossthwaite flicked a glance at me, Sweeny did not, and that ended it: Crossthwaite stiffened and jerked himself away with huge resentment. He walked with his head down and his hands curled tight into fists.

Sweeny said, "Magruder, stand fast. The rest of you fall in on a line facing Lieutenant Murray's wagon. *Fall in.*"

The tower sentinel, Simmons, turned to watch from his high post; it was hard to tell how much of it he had been able to hear. The rest of them assembled with evident repugnance on the far side of the campfires, facing the side of my wagon, which stood drawn up just inside the stockade wall.

"Magruder," Sweeny snapped. "Right *face*. Forward *march*." He stamped toward the wagon and when Magruder was a pace from it he said, "Detail, *halt*. Freeze, Magruder."

Antoine gave me a glance, full of trouble. We went between the fires and stood throwing our shadows forward past the men. Antoine said under his breath, "What the fuckin' hell's happened to him?"

"I'm worried as hell, too," I muttered out of the side of my mouth.

Crossthwaite reappeared, taking his impertinent time; he carried four rope manacles and a wicked cowhide whip. I had not seen it before; it was not the regulation Army lash—it looked more like a muleskinner's whip; Sweeny must have got it from a pilgrim. When I realized that, I was abruptly chilled by the calculation of his obvious preparation.

Sweeny said in his dead-cold monotone, "Spread-eagle him and give him twenty. Move, Crossthwaite, or I'll give you the same!"

An odd, intangible stir seemed to ripple through the assembled men, like a wind through a grainfield; no one uttered a sound but I felt an unnatural hum in the air, like the twanging of a rope drawn very tight across a windy open flat—they were taut, ready to explode, and my sense of it was so strong that I took an involuntary backward step and locked my fist around the grip of my revolver.

But, according to the bewildering intricacies of Crossthwaite's way of thinking, it was not time for the explosion—and I had no doubt Crossthwaite was fully

89

in control of them when it came to that. He was the key. He gave the men a glance, lowered his brows, turned away, and fastened Magruder's wrists and ankles to the rim of the wagon wheel. Magruder stood painfully bowed outward against the protruding hub. Crossthwaite turned toward the men and said, "Mc-Cluan, step out here."

"Not McCluan," Sweeny said. "Do it yourself, Corporal."

Crossthwaite gave him a livid stare. Sweeny said flatly, "Twenty lashes, Corporal. Put your back into it."

Crossthwaite wheeled savagely and pushed Magruder's pullover flannel shirt up high around his chest, exposing the man's naked back from shoulder blades to waistline. He stepped back, squared off, and brought the whip down over his head with a sizzling rush. It cracked across Magruder's back, made him leap against the manacles, left a long dark streak, and snaked back through the air to lie spread out along the earth behind Crossthwaite, who glanced at Sweeny and gathered his muscles.

Sweeny said, "One."

Crossthwaite's big blunt jaw was set; his lips were peeled back from his teeth and his eyes shone in the firelight. Every one of us could see that in his mind he was laying the lash across Sweeny's back when he brought it down the second time on Magruder, and the third. . . .

The men untied him and carried him carefully into his tent, where they would lay him out on his belly and salve his lacerated back. When they carried him past me I tensed my stomach muscles and refused to look away. The sight of his back burned itself into me, crisscrossed with dark, oozing, welted ropes of flesh. He was whimpering.

Crossthwaite rolled the lash in the dirt to cleanse it; he coiled it neatly and picked up the rope manacles and said, "Anything else—sir?"

"Bed them down, Crossthwaite, and don't get notions."

"I'm sure I don't know what you mean by that, sir," Crossthwaite said thinly, and went.

I looked around for the girl and found her, a dim shape in the shadows immediately in front of Sweeny's tent. Antoine was with her.

I said to Sweeny, "I want a word with you, Tom."

He touched his glance to me, turned with a snap of his shoulders and walked to the edge of the mess tent. He put the pipe in his teeth and bent down to pick up the plates Magruder had dropped at Rose's feet.

"Help me clean these up," he said, handing them to me.

I began to scrub them out with sand, handed them to him one at a time, and watched him swirl them around in the dishpan rinse-water. I said, "You had no right to do that."

"Didn't I?"

"Tom, you're only making things worse. This situation is already too tough for these men to handle."

"Then I've just got to make the men tougher, haven't I?"

"Rubbish. Not all men have the same breaking point."

"There's no limit to what a man can endure, if he has to. I've got to teach them that before it's too late."

"You're trying to tell me you maimed that man for his own good? It won't wash, Tom. He insulted your Indian girl—all right. You can't expect him to love

91

Indians, the fix he's in. Damn it, if you want a man to be a good soldier you've got to treat him like one. Which is something I never thought I'd have to say to *you*."

Sweeny stacked the plates and removed his pipe from his mouth. "Courage," he said, "is a fortress, Ed, and there is no room in it for weaknesses, no matter what sort. If I've turned into a tyrant out here it's because I've been set over cowards who understand no other kind of authority—and if they learn to hate me enough, it may make fighters out of them."

"I wish I could believe you," I said softly.

"Then what is it you do believe?"

"I don't know—not yet."

He turned half-away and brooded toward the wagon. "You'll reach your own conclusions, then. I'm sick of arguing with you."

I could feel the anger rising in me; I trembled to control it. "You've gone sour as vinegar," I said, clenched. "Have you taken a good hard look inside yourself lately?"

"You can go fuck yourself, Ed. I'm ass-deep in people questioning my judgment without you horning in too. Do I have to tell you we are still part of the Second Infantry Regiment? That this regiment served under Mad Anthony Wayne in the Revolution, fought the British with distinction in the War of 1812; fought Creeks and Seminoles in 1836 and whipped the enemy in the Mexican War? I represent *that,* don't I? And these men represent me? Survival is morale—and morale is pride! If I can't give them pride in anything else, I'll give them the pride to stand up and hate me in the open, and maybe it'll save their lives."

"You can't distort the shape of a man's soul like that to make him conform with your own picture of things, Tom."

"The hell I can't. A man who comes into the service becomes the property of the government of the United States of America. I can do any damn thing with them that pleases me—and it pleases me to try to keep them alive."

"They're conscripts, Tom—they didn't ask for this."

"Neither did I—neither did you." He had been facing the wagon; now he turned back to give me the full weight of his stare. "How can I put an end to this? I can't fight you too, Ed—I've got to hobble you. What's your date of rank?"

"March 7th, 'Forty-eight. You know it perfectly well."

"Yes. And mine is March 3rd of the same year. Which means you're the subordinate officer here, Ed. You'll take orders from me as long as you're on this post just as if I were a brigadier or a lieutenant-general. Now good night to you."

He left me with his plunging stride and I stood rooted to the spot, staring at his retreating back until he wrenched the tent-flap savagely aside and charged inside. Within moments the girl's shadow appeared alongside the tent. My eyes followed the lines of her body as she bent over to slip inside, and then I broke loose and began to walk numbly toward my tent—and Crossthwaite materialized from beyond the mess tent.

I let him come up. I said in a low voice, "You heard us?"

"The whole thing, Lieutenant. Maybe now you see what I tried to tell you."

"We're all under an awful strain, Crossthwaite."

"Ain't no excuse for what happened to Magruder, though—is it, sir."

"You're leading up to something. What is it?"

"I don't want to say this, Lieutenant, and you don't

want to hear it, but it's got to be. These men are just about ready to let go on him. And when they do, Lieutenant, they'll let go on you too, if you ain't spoke up beforehand to let 'em know you on their side."

"You're talking mutiny, soldier."

"Don't much matter what you want to call it, Lieutenant. But they're bound to calculate anybody who ain't with 'em's against 'em. They can't take any more of this."

"*They,* Crossthwaite—or you?"

"I don't follow you, sir."

"The hell you don't. Those men do what you tell them to do. They follow your lead. If there's mutiny it will be your responsibility, not theirs."

"What the hell—do you think I'm the only one's got a grievance, Lieutenant? Most of these boys been hurt by him a lot worse'n I have."

"No doubt. But they won't make a move without you. Which puts it up to you to keep the lid on them."

"I ain't sure how much longer I can do that, sir," he said. "I don't care whether you believe that or not, it's a fact. I will admit to this much—if they let go on Mister Sweeny, I ain't going to stand up and try to stop them."

"You mean you'd stand aside and watch."

"I mean I won't take his side against theirs."

"Then you're a coward, worse than the rest."

He shrugged. "I never ran away from a fight in my life, Lieutenant. You won't rile me by callin' me names like that."

"Just keep the lid on them, Crossthwaite. We'll get out of this yet."

"Not with that fucking bastard giving the orders. Now which side you on, Lieutenant?"

I drew myself up. "We'll talk about it again."

94

"You ain't got much time to decide."

"I'll decide. In the meantime do as I told you."

"How long?"

"As long as it takes, Corporal."

"You're an officer. You can put him under arrest and assume command."

"And answer to a court-martial if I'm wrong."

"Then you got a choice, ain't you, Lieutenant? Either you put Mister Sweeny under arrest and take command yourself, or you do nothing and the boys let go on Mister Sweeny, and maybe a lot of the boys get hanged by the neck for mutiny. You want that on your conscience? You think about that, Lieutenant, and you decide. We'll have your answer tomorrow night, hear?"

"I ought to lock you up right now," I said.

"You can't afford to." He turned on his heel and disappeared into the night.

SIX

The storehouse of weathered gray wood stood askew, unbalanced by its new addition, at the north end of the parade ground near the old mess tent. Since yesterday's cannibalization it was virtually the only remaining wooden structure on the post, excepting the four-pole frames that supported the thatched tent-shelters, and the stockade itself. So that the place had a look of fragile impermanence when you were inside it: the stockade, so high and formidable from without, was only a false front, concealing a few dozen canvas tents and great empty patches of dust. To me this quality of physical fraudulence gave alarming emphasis to the precariousness of Sweeny's command, the threadbare balance of my own divided loyalties.

Sweeny stood by the open storehouse door, holding the key to the padlock while the men brought forth sacks and tins of food for the morning mess. He locked up deliberately behind them but did not move away from the building; it was as if he felt the need to stand near its sturdy, reassuring solidity.

And, in fact, he looked as though he needed every bit of strength it could lend him. He was wasted down to skin and bones, his eyes unnaturally bright, his young face deeply lined and trenched by fever and exhaustion. I watched him from a neutral distance; I had to speak with him but did not wish to approach him in front of the men. All of them hung on the raw verge of fury—impossible to tell what might detonate them. At one point I was certain the moment had come: McCluan, mixing flour in a bowl, suddenly overturned the bowl and flung it to the ground—and all of us clearly saw the maggots crawling in the mess. But Crossthwaite, after a smoldering glance thrown my way, only said, "You got the wrong flour, you damn fool—that's the old batch." Listlessly the others turned away. McCluan walked to the storehouse and Sweeny opened the door for him. He went in and got one of the new sacks of flour I had brought, and Sweeny locked up behind him; at no time did they exchange a single word.

It was not until after the morning mess that I had a chance to get Sweeny alone. But in the meantime we had a visitor. The sentinel's hail brought us to the gate and when Crouch opened up, we saw a delegation of Yumas outside—a half dozen breechclouted braves and Pascual himself, wizened and sober-faced, wearing an officer's cast-off dressing gown. There was the customary rigamarole of formal greetings, not unlike the protocol exchanged at great length by diplomats at embassy courts; during the flowery Spanish preambles, Pascual expressed his happiness to see Antoine and me again. But the tone of his greeting was cooler than usual; his smile was without menace, but I felt a chill. Pascual was a fierce, proud old man, and neither his age nor his infuriating giggle concealed the underlying seriousness of his visit. Sweeny invited him inside; he came, leaving his warriors outside, and squatted on the ground to eat with us. He tugged at the flap of skin that sagged beneath his jaw and in due deliberate course he came around to the reason for his call on us. It seemed he had received word that a raiding war party of Yavapais had been sighted on its way downriver toward our area.

Pascual's talk was even more roundabout and laborious than usual, and eventually we learned the reason for his excessive formality: he had come to ask for help, and that was a thing that could not be done straight-out. The request was couched in indirect, face-saving, and fractured Spanish. "It would be very grand, was it not, if we was have the white soldier guns to fight this Yavapai devils down."

He wasn't exactly asking in so many words but the meaning was clear enough, finally; he wanted us to use our cannon on the Yavapais if they tried to raid the Yuma village.

Sweeny said he would come down to the village later and discuss the details; he reassured the old chief by forcing an obscene joke or two. Pascual had a few warms words with Rose: there was an easy closeness between them but it struck my notice that she was no more diffident before her grandfather than she had been with us. Pascual put his hand on her arm and kept it there for a long interval before he left her. Sweeny escorted him to the gate; Pascual giggled and grinned, waved imperiously to all of us, and strode away with his band of warriors.

A short while later I made my way to Sweeny's tent. He lay on his back, belly rising and falling with his breath, his hand covering his genitals. Rose got to her feet when I entered; she said something innocuous, slipped past me and went outside.

Sweeny glanced at me—his eye-sockets were sunken

and charcoal-fiery—and returned his gaze to the sloping canvas ceiling. He said, "Now what?"

"It won't do," I said.

"What won't?"

I had rehearsed what I would say to him; it had kept me awake all night, that and the memory of Crossthwaite's startling ultimatum. Now, facing Sweeny in the hot, silent tent, I felt confused, less sure of myself; my face became dry and prickly in the heat, and I wondered what had happened to my resolve.

"Come on, Ed. Get it off your chest."

"What you said to me last night," I said. "It won't wash, Tom. I'm not your striker, you can't push me around like a recruit."

"Things used to be simpler, didn't they?"

I took a long breath. "Tom, you can't be a commander in a graveyard. Do you know how close these men are to mutiny?"

He laughed harshly. "Begorra, don't you think I know it? Do you know how long it's been since I closed both eyes?"

"It shows on you. You can't go on like this much longer. There are ten of them—and one of you."

"And what about you, Ed?"

"You've done your best to push me over to the other side, haven't you?"

"And have I succeeded?"

"It's hardly the time for sarcasm."

"I meant it," he said. He closed his eyes and spoke in an abrasive tone. "Are you with me or against me, Ed?"

"You talk as if you don't care what I answer."

"Of course I care." Now he swung his legs over and sat up to face me. I was shocked by the way he looked at me: no movement in his cold eyes—as if they were eyes that had seen everything.

He hissed, "Do you want me to defend my existence on the face of the earth? I can't—I won't beg for your friendship. I only know an officer's first command decision has got to be the decision that he himself is capable of command. Everybody else may question his judgment; he can not. Everybody else can do well or badly—he's the only one who has to be right or wrong. And with the dangerous balance we've got here, I have to be right the first time. Don't you know me well enough to trust me not to give orders just for the sake of playing soldier? Do you honestly think I'm mad?"

"Sometimes I'm not sure. You've been sick—the men don't trust you to take their side against Rose's, if it comes to a choice. And I keep remembering what you said about proving you're a better man than the Dutchman. All right, you're doing it—but how many people are going to have to die before you're satisfied you've proved your point? It isn't just a game, Tom."

He leaned forward, intense. "Once you asked me if I was willing to drop the charges against him. Suppose I ask you the same question right now—would you rescind the charges?"

"It's too late for that. It's gone too far."

"Then just what is it you want me to do, Ed, to prove my good faith? What more do you want me to tell you?"

"You don't have to tell me anything, Tom. But you've got to tell the rest of them. Tell them there's hope."

He closed his eyes. "There are times I'm convinced there's nothing more to existence in this world than a black desert where blind men pick up rocks and grope around to kill one another. Hope? The only thing I've got left is knowing I won't quit."

"Maybe that's enough for you. It's not enough for

them. They've been loaded and cocked and pointed straight at you, Tom. Any one of them could pull the trigger, any time. You're the only one who can head it off."

His eyes opened and roamed from point to point in the tent. I said, "It wouldn't hurt to lie to them. Tell them reinforcements are on the way. It could be the truth—but even if it isn't, it'll give them something to hope for. Right now they've got nothing at all. Their only chance is to get away from here—and they know they'll have to kill you to do that."

"They're soldiers. I won't pamper them, I won't patronize them with false hopes."

I had a temper that was slow to come. But I felt it welling inside me, as it had the night before; I said in a voice that rose unreasonably, "You're a fool, Tom—you're sick in the head. You'll kill them all, and yourself with them. For God's sake bend a little!"

Rickety and weak, he watched me from the pained depths of his red sleepless eyes. Laboriously, he reamed out his pipe and went through the whole intricate one-handed process of getting it packed and ignited. Chills swept him once, furiously, and his shaggy beard stood out, wild and tangled.

A cloud of smoke floated free from his pipe and he said, "They're grown-up men. I won't lie to them and that's all there is to it."

"Then you leave them no choice but mutiny. Is that what you want? You've driven them beyond human endurance and you've burned yourself out, you've got your judgment all tangled up in your own private demons and ailments, and now you're letting all their lives hang on your own compulsive fight against the inevitable, just because it's the easiest way for you to hold yourself together. It isn't fair to any of us, yourself included."

"Fair," he said. "I stopped expecting things to be fair when I was ten years old."

I filled my chest with air, with the strong angry stink of his pipe smoke, and let it out in a reluctant sigh. "Tom, if I have to assume command here to prevent a mutiny, I'll do it."

He did a strange thing: he nodded his head, not visibly ruffled, and he said, "At least you've made up your mind. I was afraid you never would."

"That's not an answer," I said, and began to press him for one, but I never got a chance to hear his reply. There was a loud hail from the gate, and boots came toward the tent on the run, crunching. I wheeled outside with Sweeny on my heels.

Crossthwaite said, "It's Yaeger—" but he didn't have to say more than that; Crouch had opened the gate and Yaeger was hurrying forward on stumpy legs, a squat figure with a red spade beard and angry blue eyes.

The men gathered, hanging back in fear and sickness. Sweeny said, when Yaeger came up, "What's the matter?" And Yaeger stopped to catch his breath.

Finally he said, "They got Jim Quay and three of his herders."

"Who did? Talk sense, Lou."

Yaeger, who was a partner in the ferryboat operation and a hard enough man in his own right, was not much of a talker; he had to muster his thoughts. "Three, four miles west, right on the edge of the dunes. One of my boys found the bodies an hour ago. Quay and three of his Mexican herders. They taken eight hundred head across yesterday, aiming for Diego. You knowed Jim

103

Quay, Tom—it was his fourth trip acrosst. He's dead out there."

Antoine Leroux came out of the knot of troopers and said, "Innuns done this, Lou?"

Yaeger turned toward him. "Had to be. Milhaus told me they heads was bust in. War clubs—*toketas*."

"What about the sheep?" Leroux said.

Sweeny muttered, "To hell with the damn sheep," but Yaeger answered the question:

"Scattered hell to breakfast. I reckon the Innuns took a few to eat and left the rest go."

Sweeny said, "It wasn't the Yumas."

I heard a growl in Crossthwaite's throat; I threw him a warning glance but he wasn't looking at me.

Antoine said, "That's probly rat. They's a bunch of Yavapai cruisin' someplace around here. Most likely them that done it."

Sweeny said, "When did all this happen?"

"Sunup this morning, I reckon," said Yaeger. "Milhaus was bird-huntin' when he came acrosst 'em. Bodies still warm, he said—he lit out back here on his horse. So they ain't got too much of a jump. Milhaus didn't stick around to count tracks but he tells me probably wasn't but eight, ten Innuns in the party—otherwise they'd of left more sign."

Sweeny said, "What do you think, Antoine?"

"Not much, till I have a look on the ground." Antoine wheeled and broke into a dogtrot toward the corral to catch up his horse.

Yaeger scowled after him. He said to Sweeny, "You aim to let him ride out there alone?"

"Antoine can look out for himself."

"These Innuns got to be took down a peg or two, Tom. We cain't have them wipin' out herders ever time they happen to feel hungry. And goddamn it Quay was

104

an agreeable gent. You cain't leave that ride. We got to pay them back for what they done, or they'll do it ever time they take a notion. Teach the red bastards a lesson. That's your job."

"Let me see if I get you straight," Sweeny said in a flat, low voice. "You want us to lean on the Yumas?"

"What else you think I'm talking about?"

"What if the Yumas had nothing to do with it, Lou?"

"In a pig's eye they didn't. You believe all the lies that thievin' old Pascual tells you about Yavapais?"

Antoine came by, mounted on his horse. He said, "Be back in a couple ahrs," and headed out, legs flapping against the scrawny horse's ribs.

Yaeger took two paces forward and poked his finger against Sweeny's chest. Yaeger wasn't a very big man but Sweeny had to throw his head back to meet his eyes. Sweeny's face was closed up tight.

Yaeger said, "Tom, don't take this wrong, but Lonzo Johnson and me took the liberty of puttin' one of our boatmen on a horse fifteen minutes ago and dispatchin' him to San Diego with a message for General Smith. I knowed it was your place to do that but I didn't want to waste the time, and we got horses down there, which you ain't. I reckon soon as the Army hears about this here massacre they won't waste no time sendin' troops back out here. Ain't none of us expect you ten, twelve men to do the job. But you'll get hep, and when you do, I aim to see these Innuns is punished. Meaning no disrespect, Lonzo and me don't cotton to the way you been friendlying up against Pascual and the rest of this red trash."

I saw the men stiffen with interest when Yaeger spoke of his dispatch rider; I frowned a warning at Sweeny and, surprisingly, he nodded to me. I had reached the point where I honestly expected him to dispute every judgment I made, but in this case both of us seemed to be thinking the same thing. Sweeny turned past Yaeger and spoke directly to Crossthwaite and the assembled troopers:

"You all heard that. It looks as if we may be reinforced pretty soon. But in the meantime we'll have to stick it out." He turned to me and handed me the padlock key. "Break out sidearms and powder rations. If the Yavapais decide to call on us we'll want to be ready."

Yaeger snorted. "Yavapais."

Walking toward the storehouse, I heard Sweeny say, "You're welcome to your own opinions, Lou, but until I see proof the Yumas had anything to do with it, I'm not going to believe it."

"You gettin' soft in the head, Tom. The whole goddamn tribe ain't nothin' but savages. You cain't never trust their kind."

Off in the shadows under the sunshade by Sweeny's tent, I saw Rose standing silent and motionless. Where she stood, I was sure she could hear every word; I wasn't certain whether she understood English, and from her expression it was impossible to tell. Her glance flicked toward me and, unaccountably, she smiled.

I unlocked the storehouse and went inside to break out the revolvers and powder.

Antoine returned an hour before noon. The three of us conferred in Sweeny's tent. I knew Crossthwaite and the others were lurking nearby but we kept our voices down.

Antoine said, "I found the bodies, no trouble. A batch of Yaeger's people showed up and took care of the buryin'. That fella Milhaus didn't see as much as he should

106

of—I calculate they was maybe twenty, twenty-five In-nuns done it."

Sweeny said, "Yumas?"

"Yavapais," replied Antoine, and I saw Sweeny slump ever so slightly—relieved. He had, after all, not been quite as sure of his Yumas as he had pretended.

Antoine said, "They on foot but they move fast. Could be thirty mile away by now, any direction."

"Not if they took any number of sheep with them," I observed.

Antoine shrugged. "I didn't see no sign they made off with more'n one or two head."

"But why attack the herders if they didn't mean to steal sheep?"

"If that was all they'd wanted, Lieutenant, they wouldn't of had to kill nobody. Quay'd of give them a few animals, all's they had to do was ask."

"Maybe they didn't know that?"

"Naw. Shee-yit, they seen whites before. The way I piece it out, you got no more than three, four blooded Yavapai bucks—the rest is kids, out on their first raid. Out to prove their manhood, never mind stealing sheep." He turned toward Sweeny and added, mild and dry, "I rise to remark, Tom, it ain't unlikely they gonna hit us next."

I said, "The fort?"

"Makes sense, don't it? They hit the fort, it proves they got plenty *cojones*, which is the whole point of it. Like when a kid throws a snowball at a grown-up and runs lak hell—he don't aim to knock nobody down, he's just fixin' to show he got balls. I don't say they gonna fight a pitched battle. Just hit fast and run."

"Something to hink about," Sweeny murmured. I looked at him, and felt sudden alarm. He was swaying on his feet; his face was pallid, his eyes seemed slightly out of focus. But he seemed to fasten his will around him like an iron hoop in the few instants I watched him. He drew himself up, rock-steady, and said in a voice full of strength, "You're probably right, Antoine. We'd better get set for it, just in case."

I stood on the parade ground in the blast of sun. Sweeny was lining the men up by the storehouse, talking to them. Magruder was up in the tower, pulling sentry duty; and God alone knew how he had dragged himself up that ladder, with his back whipped raw. Knorth, dragging his ball and chain, moved back and forth at the gate with the aimless, angry restlessness of a man in too much anguish to stand still. The rest of them stood in a double rank, Crossthwaite out front. Rose hovered not far away, between tents, half-hidden in the shade—pretty, vigilant, unobtrusive, but always startling by her very presence. Antoine hunkered by the storehouse clearing the flash-holes of his revolver cylinders with a piece of wire, and methodically capping each nipple with clean fulminates. I wondered if I should take the same precaution; the weight of the big dragoon revolver was an attention-drawing burden on my flank.

In the men's faces I could see a new toughness—they had been condemned, now they saw reprieve in sight. But I saw with dismal clarity that even if Yaeger succeeded in alarming the general and bringing the Army back to Yuma Crossing, it could prove a badly mixed blessing. All Yaeger's crowd wanted was an excuse to bring the Army down on these poor Yumas.

My mind was not a quick one; it always took me time to break loose of an old concept and grapple onto a new one. But I didn't get time. On the tower Magruder filled his lungs with air and bellowed some hysterical word; I could not make it out, but the ring of his voice drew the attention of us all. And then there was a gunshot somewhere outside—the deep, fuzzy boom of a musketoon, and a hissing spray of arrows that arched up over the stockade and looped toward the ground. The men scattered, kicking up dust; Magruder ducked below the parapet, still yelling; and the rest of us broke into a run toward the wall.

SEVEN

I went up the ladder scrambling, on Antoine's heels.
Magruder was crouched against the inside of the log
perimeter, his face white.

The strong sun slanted down across the tawny earth;
I saw brown shapes flitting between clumps of brush.
A musketoon roared and I picked up its smoke-puff in
the corner of my vision. Antoine's revolver roared, hard
by my ear.

I heard Sweeny shouting orders. The men swarmed
into their positions and started to shoot before they
fairly had time to find targets; the staccato racket ran
along the top of the stockade like a string of Chinese
firecrackers, clouds of smoke blooming from the par-
apets. The two dozen Yavapais on the slope flattened
themselves to lie in a ragged line along the ridged
hump of earth a hundred yards or so beyond our gate.
There was a lot of loud talk among the Yavapais, shouting back and forth, and I even heard one of them laugh.
Antoine said, "Just beatin' their chests," by way of
explanation. I held my fire, there being no targets in
immediate sight; reached down and gathered the front

of Magruder's shirt in my fist. "Make the gun ready," I said. "Move."

Perhaps the studied calm of my voice steadied him. Magruder blinked and rolled clumsily around the cannon to prepare a slow-match fuse.

An arrow pronged into the wood close by, twanging with sinister vibration. Three or four musketoons barked from the brush clumps. I balanced my revolver on the exploding shape of a black-powder smoke ball and felt the big handgun rock and buck against my fist. Antoine, down on one knee, was aiming and firing with methodical precision. God was a dragoon pistol and Antoine was its prophet—as if he had never slept nor eaten nor defecated nor talked in his life, but only deliberately aimed and deliberately fired, like a machine designed for that sole purpose.

Smoking arrows skittered overhead—fire arrows, flaming like Oriental rockets. I looked back and saw them strike, piercing empty tents, smashing harmlessly into the dusty parade ground. I uncovered the cannon port and rolled the gun forward, and maneuvered its aim toward the point of greatest concentration of the enemy: "Shoot, Magruder."

Magruder put the smoldering match to the touch hole. His hand was trembling and he had to force it in; there was a little spray of sparks. I was afraid he might have extinguished it, but then the flash-powder gave its warning snap of sound and half a second later the brass gun uttered its earsplitting thunder and rocked back against its chocks, making the whole platform shudder.

I was watching the target area; I had my fingers in my ears. Concussion from the blast nearly knocked Antoine off the tower; he slammed against the parapet. I could see the cannonball travel, it was that slow; it burst with a shattering roar, ten yards short. There was a burst of sand and rocks and the black shrapnel that colored the explosion like smoke. A brown naked man flapped in the air, one eyeball hanging out on his cheek by a string of tissue; an Indian beyond staggered back, windmilling his arms, his mouth sagging in stupefaction—he had been hit in the groin and there was nothing between his legs but mangled blood. Someone pulled him down.

The echoes of the explosion rolled across the slope; over it I could hear the loud, level intonations of Sweeny's talk. Sweeny was up on the parapet directly above the gate, calling targets for the riflemen like an artillery observer spotting enemy movements. His revolver boomed at intervals and when I glanced at him I saw him one-handedly fitting a fresh-loaded cylinder onto the frame. I had always tried to emulate his coolness under fire but there was no chance I would ever succeed in matching it; even now, sick and exhausted, he was matter-of-fact, icy calm—a rock, rallying figure of awe. His hand never fumbled; he fitted the revolver together in quick, sure synchronization with its rise to arm's length; he fired, and I heard an Indian's howl.

Magruder was sponging out the bore of the cannon. Flame streamed from the vent at the breech, from glowing particles of the cloth cartridge case left after its discharge. I helped him load powder sack and ball; we rammed them home and I shifted the muzzle toward a new quarter. Antoine said in a mild way, "They pullin' back, all right."

An Indian whooped and burst from cover, running away down the hill, shaking his bow overhead in defiance. Antoine had a bead on him but withheld his fire; someone else shot, and then the whole parapet blossomed with fire. Bullets dug spouts and creases in the ground all around the running Indian but none hit him, and when I glanced toward Sweeny I saw he was not firing. I said, "Let's help them on their way, Magruder," and deliberately depressed the muzzle. "Shoot."

The cannon roared; the ball exploded against the earth twenty-five yards short of the Indian line. It dug a crater; dust from it rose into my eyes and teeth.

The Yavapais used the dust to cover their retreat. I had glimpses of them speeding down the slope, dodging from cover to cover. The last half-dozen of them fired a ragged after-volley from musketoons and bows. Magruder, keyed up, said "Woop!" and grabbed up his rifle to take a shot at them. Half-a-dozen fire arrows rustled past over our heads, leaving plumed trails of smoke. The line of soldiers reloaded with paper cartridges and ramrods; I put Magruder to reloading the brass gun and Antoine said, "No need to hurry that, soldier. They ain't fixin' to come back. They had their fun."

"Call it fun," I snapped at him. My belly lurched with nausea. I went down the ladder.

The men came down to the gate quickly; someone pulled it open and they crowded through. By the time I got outside I saw them running forward to strip the dead Indians. Sweeny appeared beside me and we walked along to the place where the Yavapais had left three of their dead behind. Down at the foot of the slope Yaeger had assembled half-a-dozen of his boatmen and they were shooting at the Yavapais; the Indians disappeared into the rushes along the river bottoms. A line of armed Yumas stood along the perimeter of the village, ready if the Yavapais chose that direction for their flight. But after Yaeger's guns stopped talking there was no more sign of violence.

Sweeny and I stood looking at the dead. The air

began to fill with the greasy rotting smell of blood; attracted by it, insects appeared. There was the fearful buzz of flies around the corpses, the sickening sight of crawling insects drinking themselves drowsy in the blood. Bean picked up an Indian bow and examined it; sweat dripped from his scarlet face and I saw that he had been pinked by an arrow along his hip. Blood-stained and proud of it, he turned his flushed grin on Sweeny. "Licked the shit out of them, sir."

"What a great accomplishment," I muttered under my breath, and I heard Sweeny's grunt.

Crossthwaite came by and Sweeny said, "Burial party, Corporal—otherwise we'll have our fill of vultures and ants."

"Yes, sir," Crossthwaite said. His face was full of hard satisfaction; there was no mutiny in him now. But it horrified me to see what it had taken to bring him around.

There was a sudden outcry inside the stockade—a piercing yell that froze me in my tracks. I wheeled and ran toward the gate, in Sweeny's footsteps.

Antoine rammed into sight and spoke fast:

"Storehouse, Tom—fire arrow hit it."

We burst inside. Smoke curled from the storehouse roof, a thick cloud of it. Simmons stood ten feet from it, locked in total stasis, staring and screaming weakly. Sweeny said, "It's full of gunpowder, *Come on.*"

Streams of smoke whipped around the door, lashed by a vagrant wind. Sweeny was hunched over the padlock, twisting the key. I took Magruder and Bean on the run toward the mess tent; we gathered buckets and kegs—the post water supply, what there was of it. We carried it at a shambling lope. Sweeny flung the door open—the smoke erupted into my face, made me sneeze, and when Magruder stumbled he splashed water over my legs. It ran cold over my knees, soaking through.

Sweeny stood just inside the door; when I squeezed inside I had to blink back smoke. The roof was in flames—directly above the ammunition boxes and the barrels of powder. Shards of flame fell crackling from the ceiling.

"We can't put this out," Sweeny bellowed in my ear. "Got to get the powder out of here."

I wheeled to shout at Magruder, but Magruder had fled. Antoine came in, running, and I shouted at him, "For God's sake get some men in here."

"They taken cover," Antoine grunted. He and Sweeny looked at each other. A curling flame tongued down from the ceiling, fed by the rush of air through the door. I brushed sparks off me with my hands. Smoke-stung and coughing, Sweeny plunged into the furnace, batting smoke with his hand. Antoine said uncertainly, "Jesus, we got to clear out of here!" I could no longer see Sweeny in the rolling blackness; I bent my head against it and ploughed forward into it, feeling a blind path, coughing and choking. My eyes welled and filled, but I had enough vision left to get a glimpse of Sweeny in the firelight, weaving in the smoke; I saw him kick over the powder kegs and give one of them a powerful shove with his boot, rolling it toward the doorway. I jumped out of its path and kicked it a good swat to propel it on its way. Sweeny hurtled the next one down my way and I hurried it on; together we launched them all in the general direction of the door, where Antoine—a vague figure against the daylight—bowled them on to the outside.

Flames burst through the back wall. The wind whipped them into a roar; smoke rolled around the room in turgid clouds. I had swirling glimpses of

116

Sweeny dodging through the place with his crook'd arm before his face, seeking out the ammunition boxes—paper cartridges, enough of them to shred the garrison. I caught up with him near the side wall, where the flames had not yet come; the heat was less intense—here were the boxes. Sweeny's blouse had come out of his trousers and a corner of the flapping tail was smoldering. He was trying to pick up one of the heavy boxes, one-armed.

"Stand up," I told him, pulling him to his feet. I hacked and coughed from the effort to speak. Stooping in the smoke, I picked up two boxes and Sweeny held his forearm out from his waist; I put the boxes across his arm and loaded a full stack on his arm, braced it against his shoulder and watched him momentarily while he weaved toward the door like a schoolboy with a great, tall stack of books. The boxes on his one arm must have weighed a hundred pounds. There were seven left and I knew there wouldn't be time for another trip. I crouched to my haunches, piled them all in one stack and heaved—fought for balance, staggered, plummeted toward the door. I held my breath, my eyes ran, my throat was raw with agony; I felt the bursting pound of blood in my temples. When I lurched through the doorway I stumbled and lost balance. The ammunition boxes clattered and tumbled helter-skelter. I cut my arm against the edge of one, trying to shove myself away. Antoine touched my shoulder—I heard his quiet reasoning drawl: "All right, now—take it easy." He began to stack them up with methodical precision. Behind us the roof caved in slowly, with a monumental spray of fire that shot sparks across the compound and threatened to ignite one of two tents. A few of the men went at them with blankets, smothering the sparks. Antoine and I got the ammunition as far as the corner of the mess tent, beyond the area of danger, and I saw Rose standing close against Sweeny wiping his blackened face with a wet cloth. Where she had been all this time, I had no idea—suddenly she was here, and that was that.

Sweeny's blood-raw eyes blinked as rapidly as my own. He looked at me and rasped, "Faith and begorra."

Antoine batted a spark from his buckskin blouse. It left a brown-rimmed hole. The storehouse collapsed, walls and all. The men stopped their activities and stood watching. I sucked air, coughed, and said hoarsely, "We've lost the provisions, Tom."

"Ever last bite of food," Antoine said.

Sweeny gave him a look of bitter, simmering rage. "We're alive, aren't we?"

I looked toward the gate, my attention drawn by movement. Yaeger and some of his men walked in, dragging a wounded Indian.

Yaeger came ahead of the rest. He said, "What's all this? Fire arrows done this?"

I only nodded; I felt beaten, washed out. Yaeger turned to Sweeny. "We caught one of them red bastards. What you want to do with him?"

Sweeny straightened up and had a look at the prisoner.

"Why," I said, "he can't be more than sixteen."

"Old enough to kill," Yaeger said. "Old enough to die."

Sweeny said, "Bring him here."

The boatmen shoved the youth forward. His face was tracked by sweat and dirt; he had been shot in one leg—the only reason they'd been able to capture him. It seemed to be a clean wound, and if the youth was in much pain he gave no evidence of it. His face was thin and defiant.

Sweeny spoke in Spanish; the Indian boy's face made no sign of recognition or response, and Sweeny turned to Antoine, "See if you can talk to him."

"What you want to know from him?"

"Find out where the rest of them were planning to go from here."

"Ain't likely he's gonna tell us anythang," Antoine said, but he walked over to the youth and talked, partly in Spanish, partly in some Indian dialect, but mostly with his hands. The youth stared right back at him with lips peeled back, not even blinking. Crossthwaite and McCluan came up and watched, and after a while the rest of the men straggled in, forming a loose assembly. Sweeny said, "Magruder, close the gate and get back up in the tower."

Antoine talked for several minutes but got no response of any kind; finally he turned to Sweeny and turned his palms over.

Sweeny walked over to them, drew his revolver and swatted the boy across the face, breaking his teeth.

The youth spat. Antoine said, "Pain ain't gonna frighten him, Tom. He be proud to prove he can stand it."

Sweeny cocked the revolver and pointed it, from a distance of six inches, at the Indian's genitals.

"Now he's scared, right, enough," Antoine said. The urine ran down the boy's leg.

"Ask him where they went," Sweeny said. The revolver was motionless. The youth looked into Sweeny's face and must have seen something there that convinced him Sweeny was not bluffing. When Antoine spoke, the Indian replied, never taking his eyes off Sweeny.

Antoine said, "He says they gone back upriver for home."

"Is he lying?"

"I guess not. He prob'ly calculates we'll leave 'em be if we believe they gone for good."

The youth broke loose from Yaeger's men, swatted Sweeny's pistol aside and made a run for the gate. He had gone six or eight paces when Crossthwaite shot him in the back. The youth pitched forward asprawl; there was a quick reddening of the dust under his chest. He thrashed slowly and Crossthwaite went to him with long strides while the rest of us stood unmoving, somehow transfixed by the abrupt brutality of it, the sudden unreality. Crossthwaite hooked the toe of his boot under the youth's armpit and tipped him over on his back. The youth's eyes glazed over and a crimson froth appeared at his mouth-corner; when it stopped bubbling, it was evident the boy was dead.

Crossthwaite said, "He run pretty good for a man with a bullet hole in his leg."

Yaeger said, "That's the only way to deal with them."

Sweeny turned and looked at him. I thought for a moment he was ready to go for Yaeger's throat; but what he said was, "I'll wait the loan of half-a-dozen horses from you."

"To chase after them savages?"

"That's right."

Yaeger grinned broadly. "You got 'em, Lieutenant. They be saddled and ready time you get down to the landing." Yaeger took his men and left the post.

Sweeny let his eyes roam the men's faces. Crossthwaite had no expression at all; the rest of them looked mildly baffled: too much had happened, too fast.

Sweeny said, in a voice made husky and brittle by the smoke he had inhaled, "I'll want five men to go

120

with me. Crossthwaite, you'll stay behind with the rest. The garrison is under Lieutenant Murray's command until I return."

I got him aside while the men were cleaning up the wreckage and moving the four Indian bodies out for burial; I said, "Tom, you've gone off your head. We haven't even got food."

"Where's the nearest place to get it?"

"I suppose Juan Largo's station. But——"

"Send one of Yaeger's riders to the station with a letter to that woman you've got there."

"I'd rather take the men to the station."

"No. You're not to leave this place—I won't have this fort abandoned. That's an order, Ed."

"But—five of them and yourself? There must have been two dozen Yavapais in that party."

"We're better armed, aren't we? And they're on foot." He inspected his revolver and holstered it, and took out his pipe. "You can beg enough provisions off Yaeger to live a few days—and I'll do the same. When I get back we'll sort everything out and make plans."

It wasn't good enough; I was far from satisfied. "What good can you possibly accomplish by dividing our force in half and chasing up into Yavapai country? Every map I've ever seen marks it Unexplored."

"I'm taking Antoine, we'll keep the river on our right."

"How do you know how many Yavapais you're going to run into?"

"I've got no intentions of making war on the whole Yavapai nation, Ed. But I mean to give that bunch a sound thrashing."

"What will that prove?"

"It'll prove to the Yumas whose side we're on."

"Will it? I doubt it'll change Caballo-en-Pelo's tune."

"Probably not. But it'll reduce his support among the rest of the Yumas. Now I'm through arguing with you, Ed. You've got your orders."

"The men are sick, Tom."

"A man who limps is still on his feet. They need something to take their minds off their troubles. Now shut your mouth and get out of my way."

EIGHT

And so they left, Sweeny and five troopers and Antoine on his scrawny horse. It left me with Crossthwaite and four·sick soldiers to defend the Yuma Crossing: Magruder, with his back whipped raw; Knorth, with his head shaven and his leg shackled to an iron ball; Crouch, stumbling with fever; Simmons, the cowardly water boy.

Toward sundown I told Crossthwaite, "Send Simmons up to take Magruder's place on the tower."

"Simmons? Sonofabitching chicken like him?"

"He'll keep his eyes open. Sometimes a rabbit makes a better guard than a watchdog."

"I wouldn't bet my ass on that, Lieutenant."

"You're a Corporal, not a tactical advisor. I'd sooner lock you up than have you dispute every order I give. Now what's it going to be, Crossthwaite?"

"I wish to Christ I was dead," he grumbled. "I got to piss. Hey, Simmons, get up there and relieve old Magruder."

He then went off, presumably to relieve himself, and I made the rounds of the post. Coals still glowed in the black wreckage of the storehouse. Four of Yaeger's toughs came up the hill with a buckboard containing a light load of basic provisions; we helped them unload it into a tent, after which I sent Crouch and Magruder down to the river with water kegs. Yaeger's toughs seemed inclined to stay a while and talk, but none of us encouraged their company. and presently they left. It occurred to me the only reason Yaeger had given us supplies (aside from the Army chits we had signed in payment) was that Sweeny had killed a few Indians and gone chasing after some others. Yaeger cheerfully believed the best method of dealing with Indians was to annihilate them; he thought of them as a pestilence and a nuisance.

Returning from my rounds of inspection, I admitted Crouch and Magruder through the gate with their water supplies and barred the gate, after which I turned toward the small cook-fire Knorth had built. But Crossthwaite detained me by an empty tent and said, "Like a word with you, Lieutenant."

"What now?"

"Yaeger sent a message to General Smith about Jim Quay gettin' massacreed, didn't he?"

"Yes. What about it?"

"I reckon it ain't struck you, sir, but suppose Mister Sweeny can bring them Yavapais to heel. And suppose then he sends another message to San Diego before the general moves the regiment out. 'Situation under control, don't send no troops.' Where does that leave us?"

"You've got a hell of an imagination, Corporal."

"Have I, now. Look here, Lieutenant, we get the regiment down here it means trouble for them Yuma friends of Mister Sweeny's. You think he don't mean to stop that if he can? Was I you, I wouldn't hold my breath waiting for the regiment to show up. Mister Sweeny's gonna stop them if he can."

"Nonsense."

"You think about it, Lieutenant," he said, very soft, and left me.

I thought about it. I had to: Crossthwaite, insidious, had left me no option.

Yaeger wanted an excuse to bring the might of the Army down on the Yumas. The "massacre" of Quay and his herders had provided that excuse. And if Sweeny meant to head it off, his best means—his only means—would be to go after the real killers, avenge the murders, and advise San Diego that he had done so. Was that what he had in mind? If it was, he was condemning all of us to certain abandonment.

I cursed Crossthwaite bitterly for the suspicious doubt he had planted in my mind; I ate my spare dinner in my tent, alone with my stirring anger. If it was true, I observed dismally, the men would kill him when they found out.

The demons of this evil place were on the prowl. I uneasily left my tent and cruised the dark garrison, smoking one of the last of the cigars I had purloined from Juan Largo's stock. It made me think of the message I had sent via one of Yaeger's riders, the message to Abby. I wondered if she would be able to persuade Juan Largo to send us another wagon load of supplies. The chances were poor at best. And I had no illusions about Yaeger's generosity; it wouldn't last long, that sort never did.

Abby's face hovered before me; thinking about her, I adored her—sharp tongue and all. As I walked the silent darkness I felt her weight as if my memory were tactile: the musky smell of her breasts, the taut feel of her goose-fleshed nipples, the warm pressure of her belly against mine. Did she think about me, share the same erotic fantasies? I had been a fool to leave her; she was the finest thing that had ever happened to me. I remembered how we had laughed together and it made me wonder whether I would ever laugh again in the short span of life that seemed to be left to me.

Feeling bleak and gloomy, I came toward Sweeny's tent, intending to go right by it, but a lamp burned within, casting flickering shadows on the sloping canvas walls, and I stopped to look in. I saw Rose, sitting on Sweeny's cot, her hands caressing an open notebook as if it were her lover's brow.

Her lips parted; she recognized me with her eyes. If my abrupt appearance startled her she made no show of surprise. I summoned enough Spanish to say, "I did not mean to intrude."

"Come in. Please." Her smile, as before, was a curious admixture of shyness and bold wisdom. "It is I who intrude," she said.

"Nonsense," I said, and added, "He would want you to be here." I watched for her reaction.

She said, "I pray he comes back safe."

"Yes."

"He has suffered enough hurt."

"His arm, you mean?"

"No, I did not mean that." She held the open notebook out toward me like a sacrificial offering. "I cannot read English, of course, but this is his—how do you say?—his book. I think it contains his heart, his real soul. And I know he needs your understanding, even though he is too proud to ask it—you are his friend, he talked much of you before you came."

And after? I thought wryly; but I didn't say it aloud. She kept proffering the book, but I said, "His private journal. I couldn't betray his trust by reading that. You had better put it back wherever you found it."

Her face changed. She flipped pages in the notebook and folded it back at its first page, "This is addressed to you, I think—that is your name?"

Edward Murray. Dear Ed—If anything should happen to me I want you to have this book. Perhaps it will help you understand.

I handed it back to her. "I am to have it if he dies. He's not dead."

"If you do not read it until after he dies, it will not be much help to him, will it?" Her innocent expression did not conceal the underlying sarcasm.

She stood up, leaving the notebook on Sweeny's camp table; she went around me to the entrance. "I think you must read it," she said softly, and disappeared.

And finally, with bitter reluctance, I picked it up and began to read.

I read the opening pages—his handwriting was atrocious—and then I went back to start it again, realizing I had still been thinking about the curious Indian girl and had not paid attention to the meaning of the words. I sat down on the camp chair and read slowly. I read every word of it, but afterward there were certain passages that remained engraved in my mind.

The Maj. has ordered me to remain here with a non-commissioned officer and nine men in order to protect the lives and property of American citizens, and to keep several tribes of hostile Indians in check and prevent our Indians making incursions into the Mexican territory: in short to accomplish with a corporal and nine men, what himself was incapable of accomplishing with three companies of Infantry.... Maj. H——was enjoined to construct a strong outer picketing for the protection of the detached party before quitting us, and to leave us five months' provisions. He neither constructed the picketing nor left the provisions.... He knows of those charges Murray and I intend to have preferred against him, and he hopes that by leaving me here, the Indians may rid him both of me and the charges.

...It is true I am still under the Major's command, but I am as much the commanding officer here with my command, as he is elsewhere with his, and I think a little more so; nobody thinks of disputing my orders....

June 7th, 1851: A deputation, consisting of the principal chiefs of the Yumas, with about forty of their best warriors, called upon me today, and expressed their wish to know the reason why I was left behind, and whether my intentions were peaceable or warlike, friendly or hostile. I answered them in their own style, to the effect that it was the will of their great father at Washington that I should remain here to protect his children— the red man as well as the white—for he knew no distinction on account of the color of their skin, but would treat them all as they deserved; that is, he would punish those who did wrong, and reward those who did right and obeyed his commands; that it was my duty to prevent the red men from quarreling among themselves, or from committing any outrage on their white brethren;

that so long as they submitted to the will of their great father at Washington, I would prevent the white men from injuring them and afford them all the protection and assistance in my power; but the moment they disobeyed his commands, I would punish them with the utmost severity, destroy their planting grounds, and drive them beyond the Colorado towards the rising sun.

Big talk this, from an officer in command of a detachment consisting of a non-commissioned officer and nine men.... My youthful enthusiasms have all faded away, dwindled and sunk down into the stern reality of long, weary, dusty days, coarse and stinted provisions, parching thirst, comfortless quarters, and an enemy too subtle for encounter and too restless for peace, from whom neither spoil nor glory can be wrested.

We were left here with some flour and pork, which is almost sure to kill those who have to live on it in a climate where the thermometer averages 108 degrees in the shade and 130 degrees in the sun. I thought these barren hardships sad enough, but to be stationed here with ten men on this desolate spot, surrounded by hostile tribes, who neither want the will nor power to annihilate us at any time, and leave not a vestige of our previous existence—this is what I did not conceive of even in a dream. Nothing but fear restrains them, and nothing but ceaseless vigilance on our part can keep them in check.

...I would give more than I shall say to get a few lines from Ellen....

June 28th, 1851:...A train of wagons, supposed to contain supplies for my detachment, arrived today from Santa Isabella where the command is at present encamped, but with no food, anti-scorbutics or medicines of any kind, from the want of which my men have already suffered severely.

This train could take everything here in with ease, but as the ferry company would have to leave if I did, Uncle Sam's requirements have to yield to old Major H——'s private speculation, and the post must be kept up at all hazards. The wagonmaster says he received instructions to take in all the ammunition left in my charge on his return, to which order I have on my own responsibility, refused compliance. A brilliant idea truly, and worthy of the source from which it emanated! What a pleasant predicament I should be in if Caballo-en-Pelo happened to get it into his aboriginal head to pay me a warlike visit, and without a cartridge wherewith to respond to his pressing attentions! But what does H——care, so long as his scalp is out of danger. Whoever wants to deprive me of my arms and ammunition and leave me here, must come and take them.

June 29th: Oppressively warm. Myriads of insects swarm on every hand. They were somewhat amusing at first, but have now become excessively annoying. I cannot even keep a candle alight, on account of their interference. Enormous bats, and butterflies, nearly as large, fly into my tent and cling to the canvas, upon which I have caught some very remarkable specimens. Scorpions also are so numerous, that I dare not put on my shoes in the morning without first ascertaining whether they contain any of these fearful insects.

June 30th: I have written, according to instruction, my monthly report, and would sent it in *pro forma* were there any way of doing. I wrote however, on the 28th instant, by the train, to the effect that I have had to put the men on short allowance, which, considering the poverty of their rations and want of vegetables and anti-scorbutics of any kind, is very unjust, for I do not see that the teams and teamsters are so occupied at Santa Isabella that they cannot be employed in bringing this command what it so imperatively requires. The latter are receiving pay for this service, but the lives of mules are, I suppose, esteemed of more importance than the lives of men, and we must endure the neglect accordingly.

The health of my detachment has suffered materially, and although I have used the medicine left by Dr. Hewit when the command fell back as judiciously as possible, it is already exhausted, and the men still complain of violent pains in the head just above the eyes, and of soreness of the bones—the sure precursors of that dreadful scourge to crews and garrisons, the scurvy, which has been engendered among us by the heat of the climate and the use of salt provisions. I require the men to collect a quantity of mesquite beans daily, to pound them up, steep them in water long enough to extract the acid they contain, and drink the liquor as an anti-scorbutic for want of a better.

July 4th: The glorious Fourth has returned. I wish it had found me anywhere else, in New York for instance, but what is the use of complaining. How old Gotham is rattling now from one end to the other with incessant discharges of squibs, crackers, pistols, rockets and cannon! What holiday crowds are thronging the sidewalks of Broadway, and what an endless parade of belaced and weaponed butchers, bakers and tailors are moving down the street, fancying themselves in the martial glow of their suffocating uniforms, to be soldiers. God save the mark! A few long marches on the desert would tame them down. But let them have their day, astonish their mothers and sisters, and fire off their muskets, with both eyes shut, in the park. I only wish I was by to laugh at them and enjoy the sport. But Fort Yuma shall do honor to the day, small and lonely as it is. I feel patriotic and have determined to celebrate the anniversary by firing a salute of thirteen guns—can't afford more—at M precisely. After the salute is given the detachment will parade under arms, exhibit to the spectators—a big crowd of Indians of both sexes—the rapidity and precision of their military evolutions and conclude the ceremonies of the day, by a *feu de joi.*

. . . Great Scott, how hot it is! Thank heaven the parade is over, not an accident occurring. I flatter myself I surprised the Indians some. After each (to them) terrific explosion, how they squatted and put their hands to their astonished ears! They seemed amazed. . . . And we wound up the festivities of this memorable Fourth in excellent style, it being the first celebration of the kind the Yumas ever enjoyed the opportunity of witnessing. Whether many or any of those present will ever behold another such, the God of prescience alone can tell.

... The Indians are beginning to steal, which is a dangerous sign. It is a sure omen of their hostility. I have had a talk with Pascual on the subject, and I told him with an air of great authority that the articles must be returned and the thieves delivered up to me for punishment. At first he indignantly denied that the theft had been committed by any of his people, but finding me firm, he promised to inquire into the matter. It behooves me to be careful, and I have determined to allow none of the chiefs into camp hereafter.

July 6th-8th: Nothing has occurred to break the monotony of this Robinson Crusoe life. A dead calm prevails, like a lake unruffled by the breath of a zephyr. Solitude may, like a morning draught of cold water to the inebriate, afford the fashionable and gay a grateful relief, and the o'erwearied denizen of the crowded city may see much beauty and sweetness in its stillness and tranquility, but they, like myself would find its long continuance intolerable.

... The weather continues to grow warmer and the river to fall. The thermometer stood at 112° in the shade at 3 o'clock P.M. I begin to believe we can get used to anything, like the King of Pontus, who managed to accustom his system to the reception of poison to such an extent that at last he could swallow the largest doses with impunity. It must be very satisfactory to be poison-proof, but what a happy state of existence it must have been which compelled him to resort to such means for the protection of his life. Now, by this scorching, broiling and baking process I am undergoing, I may eventually become a Salamander, whose inflammability would suit this temperature admirably, but the ordeal is anything but pleasant. I have now become so accustomed to the heat that I consider it a cool day when the thermometer does not rise above 100°.

... The mesquite beans are nearly all gone. I have nothing but a little flour and pork.

... Today I was honored with a visit from a beautiful girl, whose Indian name I forget, but whom I christened the Rose of the Colorado. She is a stately damsel, with eyes unlike those of the men, which are small, dark, and expressive of cunning; while hers are large, wild and almost dazzling with their black brilliancy. Her features are even, and their expression much softer and more intelligent than any I ever observed in an Indian face before. But her form, which was almost nude, was truly magnificent, and would have been a glory to a young sculptor. Her carriage is exceedingly graceful, half boldness and half timidity, like the movement of a gazelle or antelope. Her sole garment was the El-thu-dhik, a kind of petticoat, made of the inner bark of the willow, and consisting of two separate parts; one in front like an apron, interwoven with a little colored woolen cord and some fringes, and the other half behind perfectly plain. She wore a necklace of shells, and ear-rings. I was much struck with her appearance, and endeavored to engage her in conversation, in which I was more fortunate than I had anticipated, for I had found the Yumas uniformly shy and taciturn (except for old Pascual). The Rose of the Colorado was more intelligent and communicative than any with whom

I had previously conversed. As she grew more familiar she seemed much amused at my dress.

July 20th: I have had some birds presented to me by Rose of the Colorado, who averse to killing her pets, gave them to me as she could not afford to keep them any longer. I domesticated them very easily, and fed them from my own hand, on the young tender leaves of the mesquite tree of which they are very fond. I let two of them go the other day, by way of experiment, just to see what use they would make of their liberty. During the first three or four days they returned regularly for their meals alone, but since then they have brought their friends, and their company has increased much from day to day. If their numbers continue to multiply, I know not what I shall do. They seem so tame and confiding, even recognizing my voice and responding to my call when I am out of sight, that I cannot find the heart to kill them.

...Without woman Paradise is a desert, and with her a desert may be made a Paradise.

...My health is so feeble that I can only eat a little hard bread boiled in goat's milk....

...I enquired today of the "gentle savage" about the Yuma marriages, and she informed me they are ordinarily effected by a kind of purchase, but a chief could choose any unmarried squaw, unless she were the daughter of his equal or superior, in which case he had to negotiate for her in a mercenary manner.

...Today Rose timidly approached me, as I was

standing in the shadow of my tent. She presented me gracefully with an offering in the shape of two small fish. The Colorado is poorly supplied with fish, but these were the best, and I accepted them with due acknowledgments. The beautiful girl asked whether our women were not very beautiful, and I assured her that they were, but that she herself would be considered very handsome among them.

...We are entirely out of coffee and sugar, and have to live on bad pork, musty flour and careless weed—the only anti-scorbutic procurable here any more. The thermometer ranges from 105 to 108 degrees in the shade. The Indians are collecting around camp in great numbers lately....

...We have tried very hard to raise garden vegetables, but it proved a complete failure.

...There was a conspiracy gotten up by some of the men to desert in a body and shoot down all who opposed them. I have blocked the game, however, by putting the ringleader in chains and keeping a sharp lookout for the others....I had the command paraded today to witness the punishment of Knorth for the crime of desertion. He was publicly whipped. It made a deep impression on the command; several men were so much affected that they had to fall out of ranks. The conspiracy among the men to desert has, I think, been broken up.

...It would be impossible to convey a correct idea of our deplorable condition, one would have to be here to appreciate it fully. The men unanimously christened it "Camp Desolation." I wonder how Major H——would feel if *he* were ordered out with a corporal and nine men, cut off from all intercourse with the world for months—except what a chance traveler afforded—with nothing but salt pork and musty hard bread to eat, and scarcely enough of that, surrounded too, by warlike tribes of hostile savages.

Caramba! How hot it is! It seems to me that I shall never get cool again. Had a visit from Pascual today—even he begins to feel uncomfortable. Asked if it was as warm in my country as here, I assured him it was not, but that the other extreme there made up for the difference. I endeavored to convince him that the water became so solid in the part I came from, that an axe was required to break it; and that people walked, and wagons were driven upon the rivers as upon a road. He listened very attentively to my account, but shook his head incredulously, observing that he should like to believe all I said but that he knew I was only laughing at him. I could not help smiling at the curious expression his countenance wore as he made this reply, which of course, confirmed him in his unbelief. These Indians are remarkable specimens of animated nature, it is impossible to convince them with respect to anything but what they see, hear, feel, taste or smell.

The mercury continues to rise steadily. The nights bring no relief now—the heat is too excessive to admit of sleep, and one rises in the morning feverish and unrefreshed. I am tormented with an unquenchable thirst. I really despair of getting out of this place, for if the Indians do not wipe out me and my little party I verily believe we shall choke with thirst, or be scorched to death by this intolerable desert. They say the thermometer will rise to boiling heats ere it subsides; I cannot see what chance we have of escaping. I expect some travlers will find our bones bleaching in this wilderness and sapient surmises will be hazarded as to whether they are the relics of Indians or whites; if whites, whether they were murdered by the red men, or died of starvation. There is not one order Maj. H——utters that is not objected to by somebody under his command, but I have resolved that I shall retain this post. Yet in this matter I fear I shall be disappointed. . . .

Sweeny's journal kept me awake through much of the night, until the lamp began to flicker on low oil and my eyelids grated and drooped. His crabbed scrawl made it hard going; still, I read it through in its entirety twice, and went back over parts of it yet again, seeking the elusive clues that might explain why he thought it would be essential to my understanding. Toward the end, the diary became jerky and abrupt, filled with wandering vagaries and drifting non-sequiturs—it charted a steady course of deterioration. Pages were filled with fragments of poems, Coleridge and Donne, quoted from memory—accurately enough, but without any evident purpose, except in patches here and there:

> Solitude
> And silence are companionship for God
> But not for man. The mountains, floods, trees, beasts
> And all the lower works in nature may
> Excite in us their proper love and life,

138

But fellowship with men alone awakens
What softens and ennobles. Loneliness
Will make a savage and will keep him such.

And it closed abruptly:

There has not a man deserted from my command.... After Murray and myself consulted for
a while, we came to the conclusion that four men
were all that I could spare. If we were cut off,
which was not unlikely, Murray would still be in
a condition to sustain himself.... When Murray
came out.... I had nothing but a little flour and
pork

Not even a punctuation mark to close it off. Perhaps,
interrupted, he planned to finish it later. But the fuzzy
disjointedness of it left me aghast.

I went back and re-read the passages concerning
Rose; Sweeny kept himself a secret from his own journal, he guarded his feelings behind a mask of secrecy
as if he expected the book to be brought out in open
court someday against him. Yet, reading between the
lines, I had the feeling that where Rose was concerned
he had not even asked the obvious questions of himself.
He didn't care to know whether he loved her or not;
her intimate affection eased the loneliness, and he
seemed to think that was all that mattered.

As for the Dutchman, there were paragraphs that
made no bones of Sweeny's contempt for him, as might
have been expected. But as I studied the scattered
phrases I came to realize that toward the end, Heintzelman had become an impersonal nemesis—not a
man, venal and corrupt, but a marker against which
Sweeny measured himself; not a personal enemy, but

a cage, against the bars of which Sweeny hurled himself with increasing resentment. The goal of justice—which we had originally sought had somewhere got lost in the fevered demons of Sweeny's mind. Now all that was left was Sweeny's compulsive obsession to prove that he could survive whatever tortures the Dutchman devised. He laid everything at Heintzelman's door, much as a gambler who had lost everything and then regained it would blame his loss on Fate and take for himself the credit of having won it back. Heintzelman had done everything short of murder to grind him down. Heintzelman had given him a hopeless job—Sweeny had accomplished it. Heintzelman had sent Sweeny where Sweeny couldn't possibly survive—Sweeny had prevailed. Heintzelman had saddled him with a squad of inept conscripts, likely to bolt and desert or to mutiny and murder—Sweeny intended to turn them into crack soldiers. Heintzelman had tried to crush his spirit—Sweeny had become more defiant, harder, tougher than ever before. In short, Heintzelman was God, and Sweeny intended to prove he was better than God.

I retired to my quarters. There was no sign of Rose, and I did not seek her out. As I drifted toward sleep I tried to fathom what justifications Sweeny expected me to find in his journal. It had reinforced my knowledge of the heartbreaking hardships he and the men had suffered; it documented vividly and graphically his own grinding disintegration; it showed his intentions to defy the worst that Heintzelman could dish out—but at what cost? It explained many things, but did it excuse them? *Did it make him right?*

NINE

Five slow days passed wearily. I had to extort another
load of foodstuffs from Yaeger, which he gave up grudg-
ingly and only on my threat of abandoning him to the
Hostile Savages; Yaeger had some kind of mystical
notion that because my ridiculous little band repre-
sented the might of the Army, he would be safe from
depredations so long as we remained to protect him.
And, in fact, there was no doubt the Yumas were impressed and frightened by our cannon, which we were
careful to discharge every evening. But still, Yaeger
and his ten or twelve toughs were better equipped to
protect themselves than we were.

On the third day Pascual paid us a visit. At first I
thought he had come on some state occasion, but it
turned out he only wanted to talk to his granddaughter.
Evidently he tried to persuade her to come home to the
village with him, but Rose refused. Afterward I asked
her why she stayed with us; she only said she wanted
to keep Sweeny's tent clean and ready for his return.
It was foolishness and she knew I knew it, but I couldn't
coax a better answer out of her until two days later,
when Caballo-en-Pelo came up the hill and subjected
us to one of his silent saber-rattling stares before he
turned around and disappeared like a ghost. Then Rose
said to me, "That one wishes to kill you so much that
he can taste the victory on his tongue."

"And that's why you've stayed with us?"

"It is what *he* would want."

Once or twice I had heard her address Sweeny as "Tomás," but now in Sweeny's absence she never used his name.

I said, "If Caballo-en-Pelo should gather the people to make an attack against us, it would be very difficult for you."

"Difficult? I might be killed, that is all." She gave me her sparkling smile and went away, superbly self-contained. I realized I would never be able to understand her.

Crossthwaite had been lurking nearby; he came over to me and said, "Things ain't fucked up enough around here, we got to have that squaw in our hair."

"Stick it up your ass, Crossthwaite."

"Listen, Lieutenant, you decided what you going to do if Mister Sweeny comes back and tries to stop the regiment from coming out here?"

"I've decided," I said.

"To do what?"

"I don't know of any regulation that says I have to take you into my confidence, Corporal."

"Goddamn it, you listen to me——"

"Keep a civil tongue in your head, Corporal."

He clamped his mouth shut, glowered, and lunged away. Under other circumstances I might have had him flogged for his inexcusably arrogant disrespect; but then, under other circumstances Crossthwaite wouldn't have displayed it. He was an opportunist, that was all. I had hardened to his insolence and for the most part ignored it, which infuriated him but made it possible for us to get along without an explosion. For he knew I needed him more than he needed me.

The sixth day passed like the others. Magruder's

back had healed admirably. I removed Knorth's ball and chain after a crisp talk with him. The days were unimaginably hot; toward noon I saw a sun-maddened scorpion stinging itself to death near the ashes of the storehouse. In the cooler parts of the afternoons I regularly fell out the squad for an hour's marching drill, which they accepted with dull resignation—it was better than doing nothing. But time dragged miserably. There was nothing to think about but our dismal plight, and nothing to do but think about it.

By the seventh day I was agitated by worry about Sweeny; he should have returned by now, or at least we should have had word of him. But there was nothing, only the occasional passage of hardy travelers who had braved the midsummer passage from El Paso across the Peloncillos, up the shriveled San Pedro Valley, through the outpost at Tucson, up the wasted Pima deserts to the sun-battered Bend of the Gila, and down the frightful two hundred miles of arid heat to the Yuma Crossing. A passage from Sweeny's journal summed all of them up in my mind: "... our immigrants, who come pouring in by this route, and whose sufferings are from the nature of the country and the hostility of the Indians such as might have appalled and intimidated any but those infected with the invincible lust of gold."

The eighth day crawled by; I batted around the fort in uncontrolled restless rage—Crossthwaite only reflected my own burning anxieties when he said, "What if they don't come back? What if they all dead up there someplace? What we gonna do then, Lieutenant?"

I had no answer for him. I spent a good part of the afternoon composing and rehearsing in my mind the plea I would have to use tomorrow in order to beg a further supply of food from Yaeger.

But that unpleasantness, at least, was spared us. For as the sun threw its last burst of light along the horizon, a wagon creaked its way up the back slope of the bluff. Called to the gate by the sentry, I tried to make it out against the red sky to westward; whatever it was, I thought, it offered no threat, and I ordered the gate flung open. I walked outside and waited to meet our visitor. As the wagon crawled nearer, drawn by four heaving mules, I could see it was heavily laden, its high bulky load covered by a canvas tarp. The driver's head rode silhouetted above, covered by a broad sombrero that flopped at the edges, making recognition impossible until, with a great start of recognition, I heard the driver's smoky voice lash curses at the team. My heart began to pound: I ran down the slope like a schoolboy.

"Abby!"

I ran flapping toward her; when I came close in the dimming light I saw her lovely eyes widen; her skin blushed at cheek and throat; her mouth trembled. She halted the team and leaped to the ground, and came toward me with fluid grace. She glowed; she held my eyes locked, came on her toes into my hungry embrace. I gave her a long, lover's kiss, searching deep, a sweet close blending; she shuddered and sighed against me. I kneaded the taut textures of her back as if to sculpt her anew; her weight dizzied me.

We had to come up for breath. She said, "My God, Edward. Oh, my darling!" And yanked my head down for a kiss again.

Crossthwaite and Simmons came down toward the wagon; we drew apart. Abby said matter-of-factly, "I got your letter and here I am." Her brilliant smile was as good as another kiss.

"I never thought you'd bring it yourself."

"I couldn't stay away any longer," she said. "God, look at me, grinning like an idiot. Slap me or something, you ugly son of a bitch."

Crossthwaite and Simmons came within earshot and I said, "Let's get this wagon inside the gate, Corporal."

"Yes sirree, Bob," said Crossthwaite. His frankly appraising glance virtually disrobed Abby on the spot.

I said dryly, "Abby, this is Crossthwaite, that's Simmons. Mrs. Marshall, gentlemen, and there'll be all due courtesies. Move that wagon now."

Dust around the moon was a luminous ring. I sat on the blanket with my back against the stockade; Abby laid her head back against my thigh. I grinned and ruffled her hair. "Still impossible to believe," I said.

"That I'd come out here? Why? I'm not a woman's woman anyway—I'd much rather be with men. With you. But then, I didn't know how goddamned hot it was going to be out here. You didn't tell me that, you bastard."

"I don't suppose Juan Largo was happy to see you go."

"There," she said, "you are wrong. Ever since you left I've made life miserable for everybody around the place. He practically begged me on bended knee to get the hell away from the place before I turned them all into drooping, wilted cowards. Didn't even put up an argument when I handed him the Army chit you'd sent me for the load. But he does want his wagon back sometime."

She stood up then and reached for my hand. "Let's go inside, Edward."

Inside my tent we strained against each other, mad, out of hand, a disordered rush of needs. I kissed her

145

mouth; she slipped her face away and guided my lips down her cheek to her throat. "I've always been too damned emotional," she panted. "It's got me into trouble before and I suppose it will again. God, I couldn't stand it there without you. Will you rape the hell out of me tonight, Edward?"

The morning bloomed hot, hotter than ever. Simmons and Magruder brought the water kegs up from the river and Crossthwaite said, "They got to be dead, Lieutenant, otherwise we'd of heard something by now."

Abby said, "You're just a beaming ray of sunshine, Corporal."

"We'll wait," I said, "until the end of the week."

"And then what?" Crossthwaite demanded.

"Then you'll do what I tell you to do," I answered.

The day seemed to pass much more quickly than its predecessors. Abby's arrival had pulled me out of my dulled lethargy; and then, too, the day which had promised to scorch the earth turned out to be not so fierce after all—a vagary of a wind wandered along the river, so the temperature climbed to 105 degrees instead of 120.

Abby said, "What this place needs is a lot more saloons."

"That's not all it needs," I said.

"I know. These men are really torn apart, aren't they?"

"If you think it's torn the men apart, you should see what it's doing to Sweeny."

I had told her as much of it as I could—as much as I understood, myself. She said, "I think your friend is an honest man, Edward."

"Honest? Sure. But too honest to be kind—so honest he destroys people. He's got to learn to bend."

"At any rate I hope he comes back safe."

"Aye," I breathed. "Let's talk about something else. I've added the back-pay I've saved, and we can——"

She laughed at me.

Sweeny did not come that day; there was no word from him. After dark I made rounds of inspection and found Rose standing by Sweeny's tent talking with Abby. Abby's Spanish was atrocious but they seemed to have made friends. Afterward, in my quarters, Abby said, "She's a real treasure. Imagine finding her out here. Does your friend know how lucky he is?"

"In his way he does."

"You make him sound very strange. I'm dying to meet him."

My riveting glance changed her expression; she said, "I'm sorry—of course I didn't mean it that way. He'll be all right, I have a feeling of it."

"I hope you're right. We're in trouble with him, but we're in worse trouble without him." But I was thinking, Never mind the Yavapais—what if his own men turned on him, left him in the desert, ran north on Yaeger's horses to the gold country? If it had happened like that, we'd never know it.

Abbey said, "What are you thinking?"

"If he doesn't show up tomorrow, I'll have to take the rest of the men out and search for him. You'll have to stay in Yaeger's camp—we'll let Yaeger have the cannon until I get back."

She didn't beg against it. She only lay back, her soft hair flowing onto her bare shoulders. "Let's not think about tomorrow," she said, and gave me a deep, luminous look.

I bowed to her. "Lieutenant Murray's respects, and Lieutenant Murray is at your disposal."

My hand moved across the silky, intimate textures of her body, feeling the hot breath of her flesh; I tasted her nipples and felt the sliding tight grip of her short-haired sheath, the warm, soft, rolling folds of her insides. She gave herself to me with even greater abandon than ever before.

We held each other close and dreamed open-eyed; our silence was filled with confidences, our communion was deep, a soft and nesty feeling, and when she fell asleep with one hand clutched in her hair I was thinking that now I could withstand anything. It was as if strength flowed from her to me, through the touch of her fingertips. Bring on the Dutchman; bring on anything.

Bring on Sweeny. For in the morning, by some merciful maneuver of fate, Sweeny and his troop returned.

TEN

"I burned the camp and everything in it except what the men took a fancy to," Sweeny said. He drooped in his camp chair like a loose sack of oats; the air around him was poisoned by his acrid pipe smoke. "It wasn't far from Chimney Peak—about fifty miles up the river from here. I have no idea how many of them we killed but the fighting terminated with fourteen Yavapai corpses on the ground and, as you see, no losses on our side. They carried off some of their casualties with them so we couldn't get an accurate count."

He seemed in higher spirits than I had seen him enjoy for a long time; yet his fatigue-raw eyes blinked slowly, his expression was loose and faded, and clearly he was trying to conceal the fact that he was living on his nerves. "We did all the mischief we could," he said. "Ran short of provisions, of course—we had to kill a horse and live on the meat for the past three days. Amazing how good horse meat can taste. Last night we camped by the river—Antoine and I drank eight quarts of water within an hour." He smiled with an odd sort of childish pleasure. His state unsettled me.

They had come in on plodding horses, two of them riding double on a single animal. The troopers seemed bound up in dreamlike apathy, bland and unresponsive; even Antoine's painful dignified features were glazed by exhaustion. But none of them had broken;

I was amazed. They had eaten and drunk greedily; most of them fell asleep where they lay. Now the five of us crowded inside Sweeny's tent—Antoine, the two women, Sweeny, and myself—and Sweeny had the floor. He was savoring his triumph.

But finally he said, "I'm fighting off sleep—I'm going to throw you out now."

The group broke up; Abby came outside with me and said, "You were right. He's a remarkable character."

"If that's the word for it. More and more I have the feeling we can't rely on his sanity."

"No," she said, with that curious positive way she had of making judgments. "He's more levelheaded than you think, and much more concerned about all of you. He just doesn't make a show of it, that's all—he can't afford to."

"He doesn't care," I answered. "He doesn't care anymore."

"You're wrong about him, Edward."

"How can you be so sure? You've only just met him."

"I could see it in his eyes—the way he looked at his men. I understood what he tried to tell you before—if he tried to keep them angry with him, it was because it was the only thing that could pull them through this. Look at them."

They lay asprawl in the shade, two or three of them snoring. Antoine had sat down with his back against a corral post and fallen promptly asleep. Abby said, "Look at them. They're alive. He took them out after those Indians to prove something to them, and he did it."

"Proved what? That he's better than Heintzelman when it comes to fighting Indians?"

"Oh, Edward, can't you see? He's proved to them that they're strong enough to survive!"

"It's all too mystical for me," I said. "All I want to do is bring an end to all this. Where are those damn cigars you brought?"

But maybe she was right: maybe it took a crueler man than me to prevail in this inhuman desert. At any rate I saw a remarkable thing in the next twenty-four hours. The men who had gone through the crucible with Sweeny talked to Crossthwaite and the others who had not, and by morning I could see a new respect in the way they all regarded Sweeny. Perhaps by leading them into action, Sweeny had converted them: he had intended it as a tonic—evidently it had worked.

Simmons was in the tower near noon on the day after Sweeny's return. I heard him call down to Crossthwaite in a complaining voice: "When do I get relieved up here?"

"What'd Lieutenant Sweeny tell you, soldier?"

"Told me to stay put up here until I was relieved."

"All right, then. The Lieutenant tells you to sit still, Simmons, you sit still till you get boils. Hear?"

Sweeny came in sight. He was very tired, still, and walked slowly in the heat. He said, "You might relieve him now, Corporal. Damn hot up there."

"Yes, sir." Crossthwaite wasn't up to smiling but there was no sign of his old insolence. I did catch a grin on Simmons' face when he came down the ladder.

Sweeny said to him, "You'll want help carrying the water up today, Simmons. Take two men with you."

"Thanks, Lieutenant."

Heat clung to the ground like melted tar. Sweeny said to me, "Well, Ed?"

"They're with you, Tom, but I still don't see how you did it."

"Taught them self-respect. They're all through feeling sorry for themselves. Morale is pride—didn't one of us say that before? Seven of us went against thirty Yavapais and we beat the shit out of them. It needed something like that—God knows what I'd have done without those Yavapais."

I nodded absently; I was working up courage to speak, and finally I blurted, "Tom, Crossthwaite got it in his head you'd try to keep the regiment from coming out here. What about that?"

"I thought of it," he said without hesitation. "It might make things easier on our Yuma friends."

"But harder on ourselves."

"I know," he said, very grave. More than ever I could see the tracks of exhaustion on his face. "Ed, I didn't know myself if we'd weather this or not. If things had gone another way, I think I might have tried to head off the regiment. If I'd been a little less sure of myself. But we've handled everything else—we can handle the Dutchman too. Let him come."

I let out a long pent-up breath. "That takes a heavy load off my mind. It wouldn't hurt for you to tell Crossthwaite."

"I already have. Why do you think he's turned so friendly?"

"So that's it."

Sweeny gave me his tired grin. "Have a little more faith in me, old friend. We'll pull through this yet."

"It won't be easy. Yaeger wants the Yumas crushed, and the Dutchman listens to Yaeger. He's got to—he's Yaeger's silent partner."

"Not so silent, once our charges come out in open court."

"We won't have time for that, if the regiment comes out now. All Yaeger needs to do is bait Caballo-en-Pelo into doing something foolish. It wouldn't take much.

And Yaeger and the Dutchman would have all the excuse anybody'd need to sit hard on the Yumas."

"I know," he said, and added in a lower voice, "I wish I had an easy answer to it."

Yaeger called on us during the afternoon, in the company of a dispatch rider whom he had met on the trail. Yaeger's face was full of cruel satisfaction. The dispatch rider wore the uniform of the California State Militia but his message was from General Smith in San Diego. Sweeny unfolded it, read it, and handed it to me. Yaeger said, "Looks like we gonna get some action down here now."

Antoine Leroux was squatting in the shadows of the mess tent like some sort of malignant mushroom; he bestirred himself and joined us on the flat, his face twisted in agony. I passed the dispatch on to him. Sweeny told the dispatch rider to settle his horse and feed himself; then he said to Yaeger, "I want to talk to you. Mind stepping down a minute?"

Yaeger dismounted, still smiling. Antoine was scowling over the dispatch; finally he edged close by and said in my ear in a hoarse whisper, "What's this damn thang say?"

I looked at him. He said apologetically, "I never learned myself to read them big words."

Yaeger had overheard; he said, "It says Governor Burnett's ordered Major Heintzelman out here with two companies of dragoons, authority of General Smith. They gonna be here within a week or so. *Then,* by God, I mean to see some sparks fly!"

"That's what I want to talk about," Sweeny said, deceptively mild. "I won't have you whipping your damned partner up to make war on these Indians, Yaeger. You're going to keep your nose out of it."

Yaeger stared, slack-jawed. "*You* won't have it?"

"You know about the charges Murray and I filed against him?"

"Sure, I heard. Fat chance you got of makin' it stick, too."

"I wouldn't count on that, Yaeger. Because if we convict the Major of conflict-of-interests, we can drag you into court with no trouble at all on a charge of collusion and conspiracy to defraud the United States government. Which could put you away for a few years."

Yaeger's face turned crimson; his mouth worked. Sweeny said, "On the other hand, if Murray and I decided not to press charges against you, you wouldn't have a thing to worry about."

Yaeger's eyes closed down to slits. "You scheming little runt."

"Just think about it," Sweeny said mildly. "You can go now."

Yaeger got on his horse and rode off the post with his back stiff, expressive of his indignant disgust. Antoine and I had to chuckle, but Sweeny only puffed on his pipe and let his thoughtful squint linger on Yaeger until the gate closed, shutting him off from view.

Antoine said, "He'll humph and bitch, but I reckon he'll come arand. Yaeger always did talk a bigger brand of toughness than he owns."

I wasn't so sure. I had a feeling it wasn't going to be nearly as simple as all that.

Abby came in sight, walking the dust of Officers' Row with her graceful high-hipped stride; she waved to us gaily and Sweeny said to me, "That's a fine figure of a woman you've got yourself, Edward me bhoy."

"I know," I said; then I shot a glance at him. It was the first time he'd lapsed into his brogue in a good long spell. His face was as tired and sun-whacked as ever; but I saw the glimmer of the old sparkle in his eyes. I said, "Something's put you in high spirits."

"Only the thought of doing battle with the Dutchman face to face. Faith and begorra, it's been a long time coming to it!" And he grinned brashly around the stem of his pipe.

But his high humor did not last the week out. The change took place, as near as I could tell, on the afternoon when Pascual paid us a visit. The old man spent half an hour in earnest private conversation with his granddaughter, after which he came away and spoke softly, with unusual sobriety, with Sweeny. Ordinarily Pascual was an easygoing, cheerful old man, with human frailties written frankly in his creased features; today, though, his face was long with gravity, and when he departed, Sweeny looked alarmed and crestfallen. I tried to learn the cause of it but he wouldn't confide in me; he went off to his tent with Rose.

During the next few days the two of them spent much more time alone together than usual; Sweeny pretty much left the running of the post to me. Abby said, "I'm worried about those two," and I had no answer to give her.

It all became clear on the day before the Dutchman's scheduled arrival. Abby and I were outside the gate, walking hand-in-hand along the rim of the bluff, enjoying what small breeze there was; we turned our steps back toward the post, and saw the gate open enough to allow a pedestrian to pass through. Rose appeared, carrying a few belongings in a cloth, and Sweeny emerged from the gate behind her. She turned and they spoke, and then she came away from the gate, leaving Sweeny there with his uplifted hand shading his eyes.

We met her on her way down the trail and I said, "What's this, Rose? You're not leaving us?"

"I must," she said. She did not seem reluctant to stop and talk with us, but her face was sad, full of regret and a faraway wistfulness.

I said, "Is it because of the soldiers coming?"

She nodded unhappily. "My grandfather has talked with the sun and the river, and he has decided I cannot stay."

"And what about Tomás? What has he decided?"

"He agrees with my grandfather," she murmured. "And of course he is right."

"Well," I said awkwardly, "we'll still be seeing you often, I hope."

"Perhaps," she said politely, not believing it. Her face was composed.

Abby said, "I wish you all good things, *querida* Rose," in her comical Spanish, and even Rose smiled before she nodded to us and went on down the bluff toward the village.

"Poor thing," Abby said. "Poor thing."

We walked back to the gate; Sweeny stood just outside, watching the girl diminish in the distance. I said, "It's rotten, Tom. I'm damned sorry. I know she's pretty deep in your guts."

He put his pipe in his mouth. "Yes," he said, "she is." He turned inside and left us.

It was a thing he hated to do, of course. But I got the feeling there was a part of him that reveled in it. He would take a kind of pleasure from the heroism of sacrificial suffering; for all his strengths, Sweeny valued his honor too highly to suit me. But then, he was a better man than I was; I knew that now, beyond doubt. For his greatness was fundamental: he faced every painful decision squarely, and with honor.

I said as much to Abby, that night in our tent; but she only laughed at me. "He's not better than you, Edward. Only different. That girl is lucky, in the long run—he'd be hell to live with, he doesn't know how to bend to accommodate other people. You may call that honor. I call it stubbornness."

"Whatever it is, it's the only thing that's pulled us all through. If it had been me in his place, I wouldn't have been able to do it."

"This country suits him better than it suits you," she answered. "I can think of a lot of situations where I'd put my money on you to do better than your friend Sweeny would do."

"What kind of situations?"

"Any kind, where the best solution is to find a compromise. Sweeny sets his mind to a thing and can't be budged. That isn't always the way to make things work out."

"Maybe," I said. "I'll have to think on it. Come here— I want to make love to you."

ELEVEN

The Dutchman and his two companies of dragoons arrived on the west bank of the river, complete with fourteen barrels of whisky in a wagon, just when a party of Mexicans reached the Arizona side of the Crossing. The Mexicans had twenty thousand sheep and eighty mules—"A nice haul for Caballo-en-Pelo if he decides to bag them," Sweeny observed.

Heintzelman, an indifferent horseman, was mounted on a huge bay gelding. He led the three-hundred-man force in through the gates like a conquering hero; his face, showing the corrosion of alcohol, kept turning from side to side with haughty grandeur as if he were seeking a sculptor to capture his monumental pose.

We met him on the parade ground. Sweeny, for a change, was kempt. His hair combed, beard trimmed, clothes dusted, he rendered a salute with his left hand and almost managed to make his voice sound cordial:

"Hello, Major."

"Glad to see you, Lieutenant," Heintzelman lied effortlessly. Already I felt infuriated by his small, unconvincing arrogance—the contemptuous conceit of a petty man who somehow managed to believe he deserved better than the unearned rewards life had already granted him.

He halted the regiment, gave loud orders to a sycophantic captain, dismounted, and came to meet us with his hand outstretched magnanimously. He didn't walk; he swaggered. He was putting on a show for his officers and it did not please him at all when Sweeny refused to shake his hand. I could do no less than follow suit, and the Major was left with his hand in mid-air; he wiped it on his blouse, cleared his throat, and said with ill-concealed sarcasm, "I'm so happy to see all of you have survived the rigors of your duties. What's this damned mess?"

He was pointing at the charred remains of our storehouse, most of which we had raked up and policed as best we could; the earth remained blackened, however. Sweeny said, with a dryness that matched the Dutchman's, "Calling card of a pack of Yavapai raiders."

"Ah, yes. I received your dispatch three days ago. Smart work you did—fourteen killed, was it? Smart work. Perhaps if the circumstances were a bit different I might be in mind to commend you for a citation." His smug smile was full of suggestion, his arched eyebrow was an invitation, but Sweeny and I did not rise to the bait, and finally the Major's face closed up and he said, "I assume you've prepared quarters for me? That tent? Fine. Kindly join me and my other officers in the command tent in fifteen minutes' time."

He turned on his heel and stalked to the tent that Sweeny had vacated this morning.

Sweeny said mildly, "Fifteen minutes ought to give him just about enough time to get a glow on. Shall we go around and introduce ourselves?"

Most of the officers were new to us; we had known a few of them before—Captain George Patten, Doctor Hewit, Major Henry Kendrick of the artillery, Lieutenant Hendershott. Hardcastle was conspicuously absent from the new force, which the Dutchman had evidently handpicked with an eye toward eliminating all officers who would be likely to give him arguments. The only officer sympathetic to our cause was the Doctor, Henry Hewit, the Connecticut surgeon who was the regiment's only medical officer and would have been impossible to replace on short notice. Sweeny and I got Hewit aside.

"General Smith is between Hell and a hard place," the surgeon confided. "He's got Hardcastle and justice on one side of him, and Heintzelman's high-ranking political friends on the other. It doesn't pay to antagonize political types when you're a brigadier looking for your second star, but Hardcastle has kept needling his conscience and I believe the General's resistance has worn thin. He's only waiting to see what happens out here on this expedition. There may be fighting, and maybe you two will get killed, or maybe Heintzelman will get killed. In either case it would simplify things upstairs—you can see that. So don't expect action on your charges until things are settled out here. After that, if all of you are still intact, I think General Smith will allow the charges to be pressed in court, mainly because if he doesn't, Hardcastle's threatening to resign his commission and take the whole dirty mess to the newspapers."

"Good old bloody Hardcastle," Sweeny said. "A granite rock is he."

I said, "Fine—then all we've got to do is get things settled here. How? By helping the Dutchman 'subdue' his Indians?"

Hewit said, "I don't believe he's got the stomach for a fight if somebody can show him how to avoid it."

Sweeny said, "He never did have the stomach for a fight. Which makes me ask why he came out here at all. He could have sent someone else."

"He was planning to deliver the regiment here and go back to San Diego immediately. But then he heard about the success of your, ah, bold foray against the Indians upriver, and I suppose he decided to reap some glory for himself. So we're going to be stuck with him until he gets tired of the game."

"Or," I said, "until he wipes out the Yumas."

"He may find them harder to handle than he expects," Sweeny said. "Caballo-en-Pelo has some of them painting their faces today. They know why the regiment's here and they don't intend to give up without a fight."

I said, "When did you find that out?"

"I talked to Rose this morning," he said cryptically. I had not seen him leave the post, but it must have been so. "Some of them heard Yaeger bragging about what was going to happen to them once the regiment came. That was all it took to boost Caballo-en-Pelo to power. Pascual's been trying to calm things down but it seems to be out of his hands now." He gave me a bleak look. "So there you have it."

The Dutchman's council of war was interrupted by the arrival of Lou Yaeger, who shook hands with his silent partner and said, "You just in time, Sam. We got a party of Mexes across the way with twenty goddamn thousand sheep and a mule herd and they beggin' for you to send over some troops for their protection. Looks lak they goona need it, too—them goddamn savages been making war noises all day."

Heintzelman slammed his fist down, full of authority, on top of his camp table. It made the canteen rock; I suspected the canteen contained not water but whisky, and from the way it teetered it was clear its

162

contents had been depleted strenuously since he had carried it inside with him.

He said, "Gentlemen, I'm anxious to subdue these miscreants before they embark on a full-scale rampage. Give them immediate and decisive punishment and you can be sure they'll think twice before risking the wrath of whites again. Now, I'm open to suggestions—yes, Lou?"

Yaeger opened his mouth to speak, but Sweeny caught his eye and Yaeger clamped his lips shut in a thin, pale line. "Nothing," he muttered resentfully.

Sweeny said, "I've got a suggestion, Major."

"Go ahead."

"I recommend Lieutenant Murray and I take our squad across the river. A dozen soldiers should be enough to make the Mexicans feel secure, and I'm certain the local Indians will be no threat—they know us well enough to know the kind of trouble we can make for them if they misbehave."

I saw a quick exchange of glances between Yaeger and the Dutchman, after which the Dutchman all too clearly changed his mind; what he said was plainly not what he had started out to say:

"Well, I'm not at all sure—but then, perhaps you're right. It may be just the thing. Capital, Lieutenant. Take your men across as soon as possible. Is there anything at all you'll need?"

"Ammunition," Sweeny drawled.

Afterward, outside, we summoned Crossthwaite and told him to assemble the Ugly Ducklings; and when Crossthwaite moved away on his errand, I said to Sweeny, "I hope it works. But why did he agree to it?"

"Because Yaeger told him to."

"All right, then, why did Yaeger tell him to?"

"Because he's far less convinced of the Yumas than

we are. He's pretty certain they'll wipe out you, me, and the squad."

"Suppose he's right?" I said dully.

"Indeed," said Sweeny.

Yaeger's men, having been given their instructions, were only too happy to give us free passage across the Colorado. We stepped off onto the Arizona landing and were met by a delegation of four Mexicans, led by a very tall man with waxy Latin skin and a seamed brown corduroy face. His name was Hernandez, he said, and he was most happy to see us—"A thousand welcomes, señores."

The flats were a sea of wool; the sheep were strung out along the riverbank, drinking and falling back while others took their places; the whole earth seemed to shift and mill, an undulation of grayish-white waves.

The stink was atrocious; Sweeny puffed furiously on his pipe in self-defense. I had brought a pocketful of cigars with the same thing in mind, and now handed one to Crossthwaite while I lit my own.

Yaeger's brawny foreman came by and said, "No point tryin' to move 'em acrosst until morning. Take all day to get them all over to t'other side. They be bedding down here tonight, Lieutenant—you got enough grub?"

"Thanks for your concern," Sweeny said dryly, and led the way through the thick sea of animals toward the Mexicans' camp on the rise behind the riverbank flats.

Hernandez and his companions were immensely impressed by us as we marched up the hill with them; they poured profuse gratitude over us like syrup. It wasn't hard to see why they felt so well protected: we were as hardbitten looking a group of buckos as anyone could hope to meet. The look of our own bunch reminded me unfavorably of the brigand troop Sweeny had sent packing a few weeks before. Half the men wore grizzled beards; all of us were gaunted down to sinew and rawboned toughness, our skins blackened by the sun, our uniforms tattered. We were festooned with rifles and revolvers and polished bayonets. I had got used to the appearance of the men but now, seeing them outside our customary solitary context, I saw how alarming a figure was, for example, Crossthwaite: his face had healed into a scarred evil mask, his eyes gleamed with determination. Certainly not the sort of gentleman you would care to meet in a dark alleyway.

I had to grin; but my amusement was cut off sharply by a sudden outcry from the sheepherders' camp, somewhere in the brush above us. Soon after, there came the sound of a volley of musket shooting. Hernandez shouted, "Those are our guns!" and stared up the hill in frozen alarm.

"Come on, then," said Sweeny in his businesslike voice, and began to run. We followed hard on his heels.

We came plunging through the dry grass and tangled brush with our rifles at the ready. Hernandez let his call sing out—and it was a good thing he did; otherwise the half-dozen Mexicans in camp would have let us have it. They were crouched in a close-packed bunch beyond their campfire, staring over their muskets in terror. One man lay sprawled out on the near side of the fire with an arrow imbedded in his back.

One glance told me enough. I said to Sweeny, "Perimeter?"

"Right now," he agreed, and I swung to bawl orders: "Spread them out, Crossthwaite. Circle facing out.

Shoot if you have to but make sure what you're shooting at."

The men deployed around the clearing. Sweeny and I crouched by the arrow-shot man; Sweeny laid his finger along the side of the man's throat, feeling for a pulse.

"Dead," he said, and got to his feet. Hernandez was beyond the fire, talking to the frightened men. Sweeny said, "All right, what happened here?"

Hernandez came around the fire and pointed wildly off in various directions with his finger. "My men say they were expecting to be overrun at any moment. There are Indians all about us—at least four hundred of them."

"Sure," Sweeny said in his dry Irish. "Well, might be thirty or forty, anyway."

"You must protect us, señor!"

Sweeny's bleak glance touched my eyes briefly and flicked on. "Crossthwaite, Magruder, Simmons, Crouch—stay here and guard this perimeter. The rest of you come on with us." He indicated the high ground above us with a sweep of his arm and led the way into the brush. I cocked my rifle and spread out a few yards to his right, and went up fast, keeping parallel, trying to watch everything at once.

Close to the top, Sweeny said softly, "Down low, now—and don't make noise."

We took the last fifty feet of slope silently, bent double in the brush. There was no sign of Indians along our path, but when we reached the top and began to sweep the brushy hillsides around us, our eyes focused quickly on a small group of Yumas a hundred yards to the south. They lay along the brow of the hill, watching us, their faces painted with bright hues; they made no effort to conceal themselves, or to run away, or to attack us. I began to feel strange when we continued to do nothing but stare at one another. Finally Sweeny said, "All right, if they want a fight. I wish it hadn't come to this—we'll go down in a skirmish line. Let them have three cheers and then the bayonet."

"Make plenty of noise," I added. "Better to scare them off than kill them."

"Fix your bayonets," Sweeny murmured. "All right? Let's go, then."

We charged, leaping down the brush-studded incline, shouting like wild men. Sweeny fired two or three times in the air with his revolver. He was grinning with fiery fury. We came bounding forward, intent on mayhem, and it had the desired effect: the Indians gave us a few halfhearted yells, fired half a dozen hasty arrows, and broke away through the chaparral.

We hauled up on the hill they had abandoned. "Hold it," Sweeny adjured. "Who knows what kind of trap they may want to toll us into. We've given them something to think about—they know we're here now and they know who we are. It may give them pause for thought. Back to camp now—and keep your bloody eyes open if you want to stay alive."

We returned to the Mexicans' campsite; it took a while to calm them down. Finally Sweeny told Hernandez to take his men down to the landing and spend the night in Yaeger's buildings—we would look after the camp. "The dogs will watch the sheep," I explained to Hernandez, "and anyhow they won't stray far from the river."

Much relieved, the Mexicans carried their dead companion away with them and left us alone by the fire. Sweeny said caustically, "Unless you men want to make targets of yourselves I suggest you put out the fire."

Night came, and with it a friend: Antoine Leroux hailed us from a hundred yards away and came in slowly. His face seemed more dour than ever; he said, "I thank we in for it now for sure. Fucking Dutchman sent word down to the village he wanted a parley with Pascual. Pascual sent back word he'd talk to Sweeny but not to the fucking Major. Naturally the fucking Major had to retaliate, so he sent some of the boys down to the village and they burned some huts. Wasn't nobody in the village, but the huts is burned all the same. You think they was mad before, you wait."

"Oh for Christ's sake," Sweeny said in rank disgust. "Crossthwaite, double the guard. I don't think anybody had better go to sleep tonight."

I said, "The whole village was empty, Antoine?"

"Yah. The old folks and the women and little 'uns went down river a couple miles, they campin' out there. Pascual went with them. The rest of the menfolk got painted up—they around here someplace, be damn sure."

"Then the Mexicans were right after all," I said. "We do have close to four hundred of them to fight."

"Dandy," Sweeny said. "Just bloody dandy."

TWELVE

In the ticking silence of the night I watched the brush clumps with burning attention; shadows seemed to move constantly, everywhere.

"This is damn ridiculous, you know," I muttered to Sweeny.

"I know," he agreed reasonably.

"Maybe they won't attack us at night?"

Antoine whispered, "Who told you that?"

"I read it in a book somplace."

"I don't reckon you can depend on it that Caballo-en-Pelo read the same book, Lieutenant."

I swallowed and swept the darkness, turning my head from side to side, trying to catch small stray sounds on the flats of my eardrums. Finally I said, "I thought Indians were afraid to fight in the dark—if they get killed their spirits are doomed to wander forever in darkness, something like that."

"Lieutenant, you ain't fixin' to live too long if you go on expecting Yumas to behave theirsevves like down-east trabs."

Crossthwaite came softly by, making the rounds, keeping the men alert; he stopped and said, "I could try to get a man across, Lieutenant. Ask the Major for reinforcements."

"He knows we're here, Corporal. If he wanted us to have reinforcements he'd have sent them by now."

"Mutterfuckinsonofabitch," said Crossthwaite.

"Uh-hunh," Sweeny agreed. "But we'll show him yet, won't we?"

"Bet you ass, Lieutenant."

Sweeny grinned. I saw the pale line of his teeth clenched around his unlit pipe.

Antoine said, "Look here, I don't like this spot much, Tom. They could hit us from all sides at once. We need something at ahr backs."

"How about the river?" I said.

Sweeny said, "I don't like that much. We'd be facing into the sun when it comes up. Military axiom, Ed— don't fight with the sun in your eyes."

Antoine said, "Maybe—you the soldier. But the sun gonna be pretty high by the time it comes up over the rise. And that down yonder might be a good spot. They'd have to come rat thew all those sheep to get at us. The sheep would give us warning."

Sweeny thought about it; presently he tipped his head back to look at the sky. "We'll have a three-quarter moon in an hour or so."

"Aeah," Antoine said. "Arand here them Innuns be just a few more shadows in all this brush. Down yonder, a big dark Innun show up pretty clear against all them white-colored sheep."

"You may be right," Sweeny said. "All right, we'll do it. We'll have to go down in a bunch, tight together— make a flying wedge to push through the sheep. Crossthwaite, get everybody together. Form on me."

"Right," said Crossthwaite, and moved off at a crouch.

I scanned the perimeter anxiously, trying to burn holes in the dark with my eyes; nothing stirred, except in my frightened imagination. The men gathered in a tight knot. Sweeny told them the plan. "Keep it quiet, now," he adjured. "When we get near the riverbank we'll form a half-circle. Get near some cover and dig yourselves in. All right? Let's get at it then, we're not dead yet."

We filtered downhill through the brush, bent double, trying to maintain security; but it seemed to me we made enough noise to wake the dead. I expected to get jumped at any moment. But we achieved the riverbank after fifteen minutes without incident. We set up a tight perimeter around a dried pool caked with cracked mud, stinking of sheep urine. The animals had stirred to let us by; we left a rippling wake of nervous baaing sheep which I was certain would bring the Yumas down on us in full force. But the night remained still—so silent I began to feel embarrassed: suppose we had undergone all this stealth to no purpose? Suppose the Yumas were nowhere within miles of us? I began to feel silly.

Moonrise fell on acres of undulant wool. The men were dragging driftwood and clay up to make a parapet. A few fast-moving clouds blotted out patches of stars. I settled down a little way to Sweeny's right and laid out all my weapons on the parapet within quick reach— rifle and two dragoon revolvers. My pockets bulged with fresh-loaded .44 cylinders, percussion caps, paper cartridges. A cloud slipped across the face of the moon and I peered into the darkness with more care—and Antoine arrived so softly that I didn't know he was there until he whispered, "They out there all right."

"Don't *do* that. You scared the pants off me."

"I count eight so far," he said, oblivious. "Up yonder in the brush, just above them sheep. Keep your eyes open, Lieutenant." And he moved on to the next man.

I kept my eyes open, but I couldn't see any of the eight Indians Antoine had found. The clouds shifted, scudding eastward; the moonlit hills glimmered. At some time in the run of the next hour I heard Crosstwaite say petulantly, "I got to piss." He went down to the river to relieve himself.

The hours dragged on; after a time, inevitably, my nerves settled down and I had to fight to keep awake.

It must have got to be three o'clock or so. I moved over closer to Sweeny and said, "This is still ridiculous. We haven't got any fight with them."

"Tell that to Caballo-en-Pelo."

"There might be a way, Tom. What about cutting the Yumas in on a share of the ferry profits?"

"Whose share?" he retorted.

"Heintzelman's," I grinned. "He stands to lose it anyway, if we convict him in court."

Sweeny snorted and jammed the pipe in his mouth. "Put that over on the Dutchman and I'll believe you're Daniel Webster."

Antoine said, very mild, "Heads up. Here they come."

They came furtively, bent low, using the sheep for cover. It was easy enough to see where they were by the disturbances among the flock. Arrows began to arc toward us.

"Dig in and wait," Sweeny said firmly. "The closer they come the harder they are to miss."

"Mutterfuckinsonsofbitches," said Crossthwaite. He grinned at me. "Aw, hell, I never reckoned I'd make old bones anyway."

172

Arrow shafts skittered along the clay; a good many went high and plopped into the river. It prompted Magruder to remark, "Good thing they don't shoot very straight."

"They don't have to if they shoot often enough," Crossthwaite replied, and asked coolly, "All right if we start stirrin' up them sheep now, Lieutenant?"

"All right," Sweeny said. *"Scatter 'em!"* And blazed away with his dragoon, firing six rapid ones into the air. The racket was stunning, deafening. It crazed the startled sheep; they reared and pitched in all directions. We got up a lusty fusillade and managed to keep it going long enough to put it into the thick heads of the sheep that all the noise was coming from one direction; finally, accordingly, the sheep crowded away from us, leaving the flats open before us in a semicircle reaching down to the river.

"Like the waters of the Red Sea," Sweeny said with evident satisfaction. "They'll have to cross that to get at us—reload, now."

We could hear voices out there. Antoine said, "Appears somebody got trampled."

The moon was directly overhead. It made a fair light for shooting. I glimpsed a long-haired head among the sheep and balanced my sights on it, but it dropped from view before I could squeeze off a shot. Arrows volleyed overhead; several pronged into the clay inside our circle and Magruder said, "They're gettin' better."

"They ought to," Crossthwaite said, "with all the practice we're giving them."

Antoine said, "Shut up. Get ready, now—they ain't got many arrows among 'em and pretty soon now they gonna come at us with clubs."

It dampened the skittish sense of near-hysteria; there were no more callow jokes. Feeling profoundly

173

depressed, I reloaded the spent chambers of my revolver, flicked my glance along the tiny line of our defenses, and made myself as ready as I could. Sweeny was talking in a calm, steady voice, not saying anything important, just easing the men's nerves, as you might talk to a nervous horse to soothe it. But I heard Simmons say in his squeaky tenor voice, "I can't see anybody. I wish to God they'd show themselves."

Nothing to see but a heaving morass of woolly sheep. The clear horseshoe strip of ground around our perimeter had stretched to a width of eighty or a hundred feet; the Yumas would have to come across that to reach us. We kept up a steady pepper of firing to keep the sheep back. Heintzelman, across the river, couldn't help but hear the noise; yet there was no sign of help. I cursed the Dutchman under my breath with a steady vicious stream of obscene invective.

Arrows clattered down here and there, but not many. The Yumas had a handful of old muskets but they were too canny to use them at night: the muzzle-flashes would make ideal targets for our guns. How many were out there? The whole tribe? It wasn't hard to envision: and repeating revolvers or no, we had no chance against four hundred clubs. Sweat ran down into my eyes, down my armpits and crotch, down the palms of my hands, down into my mouth from my upper lip. Strain drew me taut as a bowstring—but I kept hearing the steady calm of Sweeny's level voice: "Easy, now, gentle down, just let them be coming to us. Plenty of time to pick your targets when they show themselves. Just easy and gentle, now."

I glanced at the sky. A mass of cloud scudded toward the moon. It touched the edge—and Antoine said, "They'll be comin' now."

Tendrils of cloud masked off part of the moon; shadows deepened, and the Yumas rose from the ground and began to shout.

"Targets of opportunity," Sweeny said. "Fire."

We poured on a terrible concentration of bullets from our tiny circle. An Indian sprang to his feet and rushed forward into the open, one of many, a club lifted above his head, yelling at the top of his lungs like the rest; I leveled my sights and pulled trigger. The revolver kicked my hand back, a lance of flame streamed forward, and the tall warrior fell with the quick, spineless looseness of instant death. The thunder of gunfire was intense; as I picked targets and fired, a corner of my mind made a rapid count of the dark shapes looming before us—not more than fifty or so, I thought with surprise. They came at us with whooping determination but there weren't enough of them to carry the assault to our lines; four or five went down, and the rest shrank back from the awful firing. The sheep were bucking and shouting, scrambling over one another in their rush to get away from the intolerable racket. When the Yumas began to fall back they had to fight their way through the sheep. The moon came out bright, and in that broken instant of unequal battle, somehow I caught the eye of a gaunt Yuma warrior. I felt rocked by that quick silent instant of mutual understanding, of angry regret. Sweeny roared, "Cease firing! Cease firing! Let them go."

Magruder said, "We had 'em. We let 'em go. What the hell for?"

"We're not here to commit a slaughter," Sweeny said through clenched teeth. "Anybody see Caballo-en-Pelo in that bunch?"

Apparently no one had. Antoine said, "Maybe he's

having trouble fanding enough people to follow him. Them Yumas too smart to want a fight for its own sake."

The sheep had scattered; only a few remained within sight. Across the river I could see the sky-glow of campfires inside the fort on the high bluff. I said, "Even the Dutchman can't ignore this much longer. He's got to send help across—or explain later why he didn't."

"Look there," Antoine said softly. It brought my attention back to our side of the river. I saw, flickering through the brush, the tiny glowings of half a dozen little fires a few hundred yards northeast of us—upwind.

"They fixin' to burn us out," Antoine said.

"Hell," said Crossthwaite in contempt, "all's we got to do's set down in the river till it blows past."

"And get our powder soaked," Sweeny said. "That's what they want. No. We'll stay dry. We'll have to clear a space of tall grass outside the perimeter and dig a ditch. Get at it—*move.*"

The wind was not high. We had time—only just. Little gusts fanned the tiny fires into a single wide flame that swept toward us with steady fury, driving sheep before it. We had to knock down a swath of grass and brush; we scythed it with bayonets and scratched a shallow trench. Arrows twanged among us, infrequent and desultory; the Yumas hung back behind the fire line. Antoine and I dragged a heavy driftwood stump along the ditch, scratching a bare patch, sweating madly; we were still digging when I began to feel the heat of the advancing flames. The fire crawled low along the ground, deep red, crackling with brittle popping voices. Glowing ashes curled through the air; smoke began to sting us and I felt the same constricting terror I had known in the flaming storehouse. Sweeny

176

said, "It'll have to do. Fall back now." But he was remaining where he was, grunting and straining, trying to pull a stubborn bush out of the ground. I ran to him and added my two hands to his one. The roots were tenacious. I raked the palms of my hands raw. "Better leave it, Tom." I coughed and tried to see him through my streaming eyes.

He wouldn't let go. I took another grip and heaved with him. A stray gust whipped flames against us and the little hairs on the back of my right hand sizzled. The bush caught fire but Sweeny wouldn't let go and I couldn't leave him there: we planted our heels and hauled until I felt sure my crotch would snap in two. Gusted flames torched against the back of my head and I shouted something at him—and the bush ripped free, so suddenly it pitched me forward on my face. I couldn't breathe in the heat; I crawled across the firebreak, and when I cleared my eyes I saw Sweeny down on the riverbank, tossing the fiery bush into the river. It struck the surface with a furious sizzle of steam. Sweeny wheeled and came running back toward the parapet; he slowed his pace only when he saw I was free of the fire. I rolled across the parapet, dragged over by Antoine's hands and Crossthwaite's, and lay on my back trying to get enough air in my lungs.

The central body of the fire reached the break and all of us watched in anguish, waiting for it to jump the ditch. The air was thick with heat and soot. Antoine breathed, "Pray God that wind holds down." A current of heat picked up a handful of fire and glided it in a spiral across the ditch; it fell burning into our grass but Magruder was waiting for it, his blouse stripped off; he flung the blouse over the flame and jumped on it, smothering the blaze. The welted ridges on his back stood out sharply in the angry red illumination.

I brought my mind into clearer focus by an effort of will and turned a full circle on my heels to survey the camp. Men dashed forward everywhere to crush out sparks that had drifted across the break. The wind made a slight and subtle shift somewhere in the ensuing run of time, and the fire bent more directly toward the river at our left flank. Burning rushes began to fall into the water and float past us. I had a strange, vivid recollection of a painting I had seen somewhere, torchlit royal Egyptian barges on the Nile. We fell back toward the riverbank, braving the perimeter only in sprints when there was a spark to be smothered. Sweeny said, "Belly flat," and most of them sprawled down with their heads out over the lapping river—the air right along the surface was not quite so fouled with smoke. Antoine stayed on his feet, spying out flying tinder, batting it out with his broad hat. I fought it with him, and with Sweeny, and my clothes became hot enough to scorch the skin beneath. My ears filled with the sound of retching and choking—my own and others. Sweeny moved around with indifferent obliviousness to discomfort and danger, walking right into the teeth of it to pick up a burning branch with his bare hand and throw it back across the break.

Antoine sputtered and coughed and said in my ear, "Least they won't jump us now—ain't no barefoot Innun about to attackt us over that."

"That's a hell of a consolation, Antoine. You hold onto that thought."

An arrow swished through the fire and neatly penetrated the hat which Antoine had in his outstretched hand. He grinned absurdly and made no effort to remove it; it stuck through his hat like a plume of decoration.

The fire's fuel was too sparse and spindly to keep it

alive very long. With the wind pushing it steadily against the river it had nowhere to seek fresh sustenance; it began to burn itself out. It was not until I looked up to the east and saw the gray-pink of rising dawn that I realized how long we had been battling the flames. The moon was low in the west, a three-quarter disc going pale as the sky blued up. Through the curling smoke I could see a sizable assemblage of blue-clad soldiers gathering on the ferry landing, across the river and half a mile upstream. The half-circle of ground surrounding us was black, many acres of spreading black. Had the brush been thicker, or the wind more brisk—I did not have the stomach to finish the thought. Sweeny said, "Looks like the Dutchman's coming across."

A flurry of arrows whipped down from the higher slopes upon our position—a final, angry volley—and horribly two of them struck home. Crossthwaite grunted and pitched on his face and I saw the shaft rising from his back, just beneath the shoulder blade. Magruder, walking up from the bank, took the other in his thigh: it stabbed downward through the outer flesh of his leg.

Antoine was closest to Crossthwaite; he got down on one knee. Crossthwaite's sphincter muscles failed; an unmistakable odor rose around him and expanded like a cloud, overpowering the acrid smoke that lingered. Agony pulled at Crossthwaite's scarred mouth and he began to curl up like a strip of frying bacon. I heard his outraged cry and then he sagged, limp, and Sweeny got down beside Antoine. "How bad is he hit?"

"Bad as he can get."

"He's dead?"

"Permanent."

"Oh," Sweeny said. He stood up, his eyes fiercely pale against the charred black skin, stained with a terrible fury. He was looking upstream and I felt I could read his mind: he had risked mutiny and death to bring Crossthwaite back into the pale with pride and honor—for this.

I gripped his shoulder. "Let the dead stay dead, Tom. At least there's nothing more anybody can do to him."

Upriver, a platoon had ferried across; they were coming downstream, wading along the riverbank, towing two balsa rafts, one of which contained the Dutchman.

Sweeny broke away from me. "Magruder."

"I'll make it, Lieutenant."

Simmons was with Magruder, binding up his hip. He had broken off the protruding ends of the arrow shaft. I was amazed by the cool competence in his expression. "Better not take the arrow out of him till he regenerates some of that lost blood, I reckon."

"Good judgment. Anyhow we'll get you to the surgeon right away, Magruder."

"I hate to let you down like this, Lieutenant," Magruder said.

When the Dutchman stepped ashore, keeping his boots dry, Sweeny said, "Broke both legs getting here, didn't you?"

THIRTEEN

Heintzelman, his face gravely wooden, refused to talk about anything important until safely ensconsed once again inside the walls of the fort. When we started up the hill, Abby rushed down toward us and wrapped her arms around me. "Thank God, Edward."

I tried to smile, but they carried Crossthwaite's corpse past and I had nothing to smile about. Abby touched her cheek to my shoulder and we walked arm-in-arm up to the gate.

The Major halted inside and let the others go by. He stared at Sweeny and me with an expression that showed unmistakably how chagrined he had been to find out we were not dead. He said flatly, "I intend to launch a punitive campaign to crush these savages once and for all. There'll be a conference in my tent at nine. Now get cleaned up—you're filthy." He swung on his heel and swaggered away.

In my tent I stripped down to the skin and Abby sponged me; an hour later we met Sweeny in his tent. Like me he had cleaned up and changed clothes; but his face was ugly with blisters and he had a rag wrapped around his hand. "Pack my pipe for me, will you?"

I turned toward the camp table but Abby intercepted me. "I'll do it."

I said, "Yaeger's been with him all night. Hewit told

me. It won't be easy to bring him around. In fact I doubt it's possible at all. He intends to wipe them out."

"No, by damn," Sweeny said. His eyes blinked slowly in pain; his voice was low and deliberate. "No. Over my dead body."

"He'd be pleased to have it that way," I replied.

"There's still a good chance for a bloodless settlement," he said. "Caballo-en-Pelo didn't get near as many followers as everybody thought he would. Most of them didn't fight with him—which means——"

He didn't get a chance to finish it; Hewit burst into the tent, out of breath and red-faced. "Something you'd better know, Tom. We just got word from the Yumas. Message under truce flag, relayed by way of one of those Mexican sheepmen. The Indians are willing to make peace but they won't believe we really want peace unless we send *El Capitan del un Brazo*—the one-armed officer. That's you. They won't talk to anybody else."

Sweeny wheeled on me with hard triumph. "You see? They don't want a fight, Ed!"

"A fat lot of good it does," I said bleakly. "Sending you down to talk to them is the last thing he'd do. Not as long as Yaeger's got his ear."

"Ed's right," Hewit said. "The bastard wants to annihilate them. He thinks it would look good on his record."

"Tom," I said, "we've got to make a deal with him."

He looked at me. He knew what I had in mind. He looked hard-eyed and unbending. "No. You can't make a deal with his kind. I intend to serve him crow for his supper, and my plans don't include making deals with him."

Wordlessly, Abby placed his pipe in his mouth and held a match to it. She gave me a glance full of meaning

182

and I turned to face him squarely. His eyes looked like two holes burned into the skin. He said, "He's got to be destroyed, Ed, and the only weapon we have is the charges against him. I intend to destroy him in open court. Nothing can change that now. We're too close."

"For once in your life bend a little," I said. "You can have the Dutchman destroyed or you can have those Yumas saved. You can't have both. The choice isn't very appealing but you're the one who's got to make it."

His face rigid with suppressed feelings, he stood up and sucked on his pipe. "Get out of here, all of you. I'll see you at the meeting."

At the appointed hour the officers converged on Heintzelman's tent. I met Sweeny and Antoine outside and went in with them.

The Dutchman's face was stubborn. The motionless air inside the hot enclosure reeked of whisky.

Sweeny said, "Permission to speak, Major, before the meeting gets under way."

The Major's appraising glance was lidded and opaque. "Go ahead."

Sweeny's voice was not at all conciliatory but I began to feel a heady anticipation. He said, "Look, damn it, it's easy enough to get into a fight, especially when you know you can whip the pants off the enemy. The problem is deciding how to get out of it. These Indians don't want a war with us."

"You can say that, Mister, after what they did to you last night? You're crazy in the head."

Sweeny took a deep breath. He said, in a strained effort to sound reasonable, "They're willing to talk to me, Major. Willing to talk peace."

"It's took late for that," Heintzelman said, but he was avoiding Sweeny's eyes.

"Bullshit," Sweeny snapped. I couldn't help but feel a swell of pride: Heintzelman had done his utmost to break this man who would not break. Sweeny said, "I want this heard and witnessed by every officer in this room. Lieutenant Murray and I are prepared to rescind all our charges against you if you'll agree, before these witnesses, to a peace conference with the Yumas. Two other conditions only: you'll abide by the terms of whatever peace agreement we reach with the Indians, and you'll turn over your share of the profits in the ferry business to the Yuma tribe."

I heard Hewit suck in his breath.

I took a step forward, stared into Heintzelman's cross and sulky face, and spoke softly:

"The chance of a permanent peace down here is more important than the fate of a single incompetent officer, Major. We're offering you a chance to get out scot-free. Every man in this tent knows the truth, but even so it's your only chance to keep your commission and stay out of prison. I give you my pledge the charges will be dropped."

The Major stood with his head lowered, his face heavy with thought. But when he looked up, fear quivered in his eyes. He said to Sweeny, "Go. Go if you want to. Bring them in—and tell them if they ever break the peace again I'll kill every last one of them. Now go, Mister—and I hope they club you to pulp."

Outside, Antoine said, "I didn't never thank I'd see the day. You won, Tom."

"No," Sweeny said. "There are no victors. Only survivors."

At the gate Abby caught my eye, making private

184

signals of love. I beckoned her over; the four of us went out onto the baked soil of the bluff, and below us we saw a small delegation of Yumas, bedraggled and shy: Caballo-en-Pelo was among them, disarmed, his eye-patch catching the sunlight; two warriors held him by the arms. Off to the side a little way stood Pascual, remote and splendid, erect, grinning his damn stupid grin when he saw Sweeny.

Sweeny muttered, "Faith and begorra." His eyes flashed; he grinned at me. Antoine and Abby and I stood just outside the gate and watched while Sweeny walked down the back of the bluff toward the waiting Indians. The pipe jutted from his jaw at a jaunty, satanic angle. He lifted his bandaged hand in signal, and Pascual answered his wave. Abby's warm hand snuggled into my own. Watching his tiny shape march down the slope, I felt feeling well up in my throat.

"Shee-yit," said Antoine, and grinned.

Historical Afterword

"The Indians finally agreed to accompany me to the post on the condition that I would guarantee their safety if the conditions of the proposed treaty were not agreed to. . . . My arrival created a great excitement as nobody could account for my bringing in four hundred savage warriors, armed with their bows and arrows, clubs and spears. The war is probably ended—we will know more when the treaty is ratified."

Thus in his own laconic summary did Sweeny conclude his statement of the events at the Yuma Crossing in 1851.

Almost all the incidents narrated in this novel did take place in fact. Obviously I have manufactured the dialogue and, to some extent, the characterizations. Murray, the narrator, was a real person, as were almost all the other characters in this book, Indian and white alike. (Abby Marshall and Juan Largo are composites of several historical persons; there are no other important fictitious characters in the book; and I might add for the benefit of the skeptical that "Rose of the Colorado" was a very real person.)

Sweeny's diary, on which much of this novel is based,

appeared in bits and pieces in various publications over the years, and was finally published in book form, in 1956, as the *Journal of Lt. Thomas W. Sweeny, 1849-1853*, edited by Arthur Woodward and published by Paul Bailey's Westernlore Press. I am deeply indebted both to Dr. Woodward and to Mr. Bailey for their kind permission to quote liberally from the diary, as I have done here in Chapter Eight and elsewhere. (I am indebted as well to Sweeny's nephew, Thomas K. Scott, who has added considerably to my understanding of Sweeny's character.)

Of course this book is a novel, and must be read as such; in order to blend fiction and fact into a whole, I have freely quoted passages out of context and out of sequence, added fictions and ignored facts where they seemed undramatic or pointless. In addition to the long extract from the *Journal* which appears in Chapter Eight, I have in many places attributed lines of dialogue to Sweeny which in fact are lines quoted from his diary; but it must be added that they seldom appear in the original order, and that in quite a few cases I have changed Sweeny's wording to make his statements fit into the dramatic continuity of this novel. I certainly don't mean for this book to be read as a factual historical record; I believe, however, that it sustains an overall truth.

Edward Murray served as a Lieutenant Colonel in the Confederate Army throughout the Civil War and died on July 3rd, 1874. Samuel Peter Heintzelman was breveted Lieutenant Colonel soon after the events described herein ("This latter promotion must have galled Sweeny almost beyond endurance," wrote Dr. Woodward in his notes to the *Journal*), emerged from the Civil War a Yankee major general, and died May 1st,

880, with his long backtrail littered with questionable affairs, for which he was never brought to trial.

Sweeny himself fought the Sioux on the plains in 1855 and 1856, then returned to New York on recruiting duty; he then married his long-suffering fiancée, Ellen Swan Clark. He became a brigadier general in 1861 and commanded troops in combat throughout the Civil War, although he was wounded twice during the conflict. During the years of reconstruction he commanded Army forts in Nashville, Augusta, and Atlanta. He also turned up—the irrepressible "Fighting Tom Sweeny"—as one of the dashing leaders of the earnest but abortive invasion of Canada perpetrated by the Fenian Society of Irish nationalists.

Sweeny died at 72 in 1892 and was escorted to his grave in Long Island City by six batteries of the First U.S. Artillery.

ABOUT THE AUTHOR

Brian Garfield, whose novel *Death Wish* was made into a motion picture, is the author of numerous suspense/adventure novels, including *Hopscotch, Line of Succession,* and *The Threepersons Hunt.*

A NEW DECADE OF CREST BESTSELLERS

RESTORING THE AMERICAN DREAM		
Robert J. Ringer	24314	$2.95
THE LAST ENCHANTMENT *Mary Stewart*	24207	$2.95
THE SPRING OF THE TIGER *Victoria Holt*	24297	$2.75
THE POWER EATERS *Diana Davenport*	24287	$2.75
A WALK ACROSS AMERICA		
Peter Jenkins	24277	$2.75
SUNFLOWER *Marilyn Sharp*	24269	$2.50
BRIGHT FLOWS THE RIVER		
Taylor Caldwell	24149	$2.95
CENTENNIAL *James A. Michener*	23494	$2.95
CHESAPEAKE *James A. Michener*	24163	$3.95
THE COUP *John Updike*	24259	$2.95
DRESS GRAY *Lucian K. Truscott IV.*	24158	$2.75
THE GLASS FLAME *Phyllis A. Whitney*	24130	$2.25
PRELUDE TO TERROR *Helen MacInnes*	24034	$2.50
SHOSHA *Isaac Bashevis Singer*	23997	$2.50
THE STORRINGTON PAPERS		
Dorothy Eden	24239	$2.50
THURSDAY THE RABBI WALKED OUT		
Harry Kemelman	24070	$2.25

Buy them at your local bookstore or use this handy coupon for ordering.

COLUMBIA BOOK SERVICE (a CBS Publications Co.)
32275 Mally Road, P.O. Box FB, Madison Heights, MI 48071

Please send me the books I have checked above. Orders for less than 5 books must include 75¢ for the first book and 25¢ for each additional book to cover postage and handling. Orders for 5 books or more postage is FREE. Send check or money order only.

Cost $_____   Name _____
Postage_____   Address _____
Sales tax*_____   City _____
Total $_____   State _____ Zip _____

The government requires us to collect sales tax in all states except AK, DE, MT, NH and OR.

This offer expires 1 May 81   8200-1

THRILLS * CHILLS * MYSTERY
from FAWCETT BOOKS

THE GREEN RIPPER	14340	$2.50
by John D. MacDonald		
MURDER IN THREE ACTS	03188	$1.75
by Agatha Christie		
A MURDER OF QUALITY	08374	$1.95
by John Le Carre		
DEAD LOW TIDE	14166	$1.75
by John D. MacDonald		
DEATH OF AN EXPERT WITNESS	04301	$1.95
by P. D. James		
PRELUDE TO TERROR	24034	$2.50
by Helen MacInnes		
AN UNSUITABLE JOB FOR A WOMAN	00297	$1.75
by P. D. James		
GIDEON'S SPORT	04405	$1.75
by J. J. Marric		
THURSDAY THE RABBI WALKED OUT	24070	$2.25
by Harry Kemelman		
ASSIGNMENT SILVER SCORPION	14294	$1.95
by Edward S. Aarons		

This offer expires 1 July 81   8400-2